SHE FADES
AWAY

About the Author

Michael Carroll has been called one of the "great new writers" of his generation. He was a contributor to *Shiver!* and *Chiller*, two collections of ghost stories published by Poolbeg. He is the author of *The Last Starship* and *Moonlight*. Michael Carroll is married and lives and works in Dublin.

SHE FADES AWAY

MICHAEL CARROLL

Dark Shadows

POOLBEG

Published 1996
by Poolbeg Press Ltd
123 Baldoyle Industrial Estate
Dublin 13, Ireland

© Michael Carroll 1996

The moral right of the author has been asserted.

A catalogue record for this book is available from the British Library.

ISBN 1 85371 621 9

Cover illustration by Michael Mascaro
Cover design by Poolbeg Group Services Ltd
Set by Poolbeg Group Services Ltd in Times 11.5/14
Printed by The Guernsey Press Ltd,
Vale, Guernsey, Channel Islands.

For my Parents

PROLOGUE

It waited. That was all that it could do. Time was strange, unordered, chaotic, but waiting wasn't so hard.

It was vaguely aware that time should be more organised. Things happened one after the other, cause and effect, action and reaction. But . . . not now.

Now it drifted, growing weaker and stronger as unknown forces tugged at it. It remembered a face. An old man, kindly and smiling. But the face seemed wrong, out of place. Was the old man from a long time ago, it wondered, or from yesterday?

Time was strange, and waiting was all the more strange for the lack of regular events. Day melded into night without notice, years passed more quickly than weeks, months seemed to occur simultaneously.

It knew, somehow, that it would not have to wait forever. Though it often felt that it already had.

CHAPTER ONE

"Here he comes!" Mairéad said, her voice a screeching whisper with excitement.

Next-door neighbours Mairéad and Julie sat on the wall separating their front gardens, their favourite meeting place from where they could watch the world go by and still not have far to go if it started to rain. They had been friends for as long as they could remember, and were so close that – despite their different appearances – people often mistook them for sisters. But in the last couple of years, their friendship had changed slightly: before, they had shared everything and neither begrudged the other anything; but now, when it came to matters of love, there was a friendly but strong rivalry between them.

Julie glanced down the street in as casual a manner as she could. Striding along, with his hands in his pockets, was Craig Kipling. He had a carefree saunter, though Julie could tell that Craig had seen them and was too cool to let on.

"God, he's *gorgeous*!" Mairéad said.

Julie whispered fiercely under her breath. "Shut up! He'll hear you!"

They kept silent as Craig approached. "Morning, girls!" he said, giving them a quick wink.

They watched him walk away.

"Did you see that?" Mairead asked. "He winked at me!"

Julie gave her a playful shove. "He did not, you idiot, he winked at *me*!"

Mairead sighed. "Do you think he's ever going to ask me out?"

Julie laughed. "No, I'm not going to let him."

"Hah! As if he'd go out with *you!*"

Julie tossed back her head and looked down her nose at Mairead in mock snobbery. "And why shouldn't he? Doesn't he deserve the best?"

"That's what I mean."

Julie sighed. She knew she wasn't as good-looking as Mairead. Her friend was tall and slim, with long red hair and brilliant green eyes, whereas Julie was shorter, with dark blonde hair and brown eyes. Plus, Julie said to herself, I could do with losing a pound or two. My face is too round.

"Mairead, do you think my face is too round?"

Mairead looked at her. "Too round for what?"

"You know what I mean. Well, is it? Am I overweight?"

"Don't be silly. I wish *I* wasn't so skinny. At least you fill out your clothes properly."

Julie looked down the street. Craig was long gone. She sighed again. "This is crazy," she said. "We sit out here every morning waiting for Craig to walk by, and

4

all he ever does is say good morning and keep on going."

"So? If you feel that way, ask him if he'll go out with you."

Julie was about to answer when her mother opened the hall door and called out to her.

"Coming!" Julie shouted. She turned back to Mairéad. "See you later!"

She jumped down off the wall and ran inside.

Mrs Logan had gone back into the kitchen, and was pouring two mugs of tea. "Sit down, love. I've got some good news."

Julie sat down and wrapped her hands around the warm mug. "Did Dad get that job, then?"

Her mother shook her head sadly. "It's not *that* good, I'm afraid. But he met your uncle Billy in town yesterday, and they went for a drink."

Julie nodded. She knew from that statement that something was up. Her father and her uncle Billy had never been the best of friends, and Julie sometimes suspected that if her mother and her aunt Carol hadn't been twins, the families would never meet at all.

Mrs Logan sat opposite Julie, and looked her straight in the eye. "Billy and Carol are going to Madrid for two weeks, and they said they'll pay for us to go with them."

Julie grinned. "Brilliant!"

Her mother held up her hand. "But there's a snag. I had a good long talk about this with Seán last night and we decided we had to ask you."

Julie sat back and pursed her lips. "Ask me what?"

"There's a condition – I suppose it's obvious that Billy wouldn't give us anything without wanting something in return. It looks like Brian's failed his Junior Cert, and of course Billy doesn't want his pride and joy to be left behind, so . . ."

Julie finished the sentence for her. "So they want me to give him grinds?"

Mrs Logan nodded. "Exactly. It shouldn't be too hard, Brian's a bright lad, but he has problems paying attention in school."

Julie sipped at her tea and shrugged. "Well, it'll be worth it for two weeks in Spain." She grinned happily to herself, until she noticed the look on her mother's face.

"That's the other part of the snag," Mrs Logan said. "You see, they're bringing Gemma and Keith, but not Brian. They want you to teach him while they're away. It's sort of a punishment for him, for not trying harder."

Julie's smile collapsed. "So they don't want me to go?"

"I don't think they want *any* of us to go. Your dad would have turned him down flat, but, well, we haven't had a holiday in so long. We'll make it up to you, love."

Julie nodded. She swallowed to keep back the tears. "It's okay, you should go. I don't mind."

Mrs Logan smiled and touched Julie's hand. "Thanks love, we will make it up to you, I promise."

* * *

The tiny figure jumped over the cactus, ducked under the swooping vulture, and dropped into the mine-shaft's entrance. The joystick had become slippery with sweat, so Brian quickly reached out and stabbed the computer's "Pause" key. The images on the screen froze.

He heard the kitchen door open, and his father walk to the bottom of the stairs. "Brian? How's the studying going?" he called.

"Fine, Dad! Nearly finished my English."

"Come down when you're finished, son."

"Okay!" Brian dug his handkerchief out of his pocket and wiped the sweat off his hands. He clicked the joystick's "fire" button, and the game burst into action once more.

Brian wasn't worried about his English, or, for that matter, any of the other subjects he should have been studying. There were still two months of summer holidays left, plenty of time to catch up.

The brightly-coloured figure jumped about the screen, dodging rolling barrels and spikes from the floor, but his father's interruption had spoiled Brian's concentration, and he forgot about the spikes in the ceiling. The figure was skewered to death, and an ominous tune warbled from the computer.

"Arrggh!" Brian muttered. "I'll never get past this level!"

He took a deep breath to try and clear his pounding headache, then switched off the computer and made his way downstairs.

He was not pleased at the news that he was to be left behind on this year's holiday.

"Aw, come on, Dad! I can bring my books with me!"

Brian's father looked at his wife, who shook her head. "Sorry, Brian. Look, if you study hard, and have improved by the time we get back, I'll buy you that new computer you wanted."

Carol glared at her husband. "Billy . . ."

"If the boy studies hard, he should get the benefits of his work."

"There's no way you're going to change your mind, then?" Brian asked.

"No, Brian," his mother said. "Now go back up and keep studying. It's your own fault you failed, anyway – you didn't study hard enough during the year. Look, if you work at it now, it can only get easier."

Brian knew when there was no arguing with them. He stormed out of the kitchen, slammed the door behind him, and marched up the stairs and into his room.

He sat unmoving at his desk for a few minutes. He was *sure* he'd failed the Junior Cert: the results wouldn't be out for another month or so, but he knew that the few questions he'd managed to answer in the exams – even if those questions were one hundred per cent perfect – wouldn't be enough to get him a pass mark.

Brian look at the things on his desk. He had a chipped *Babylon 5* mug filled with old Biros and markers. There was a stack of computer magazines and a pile of *New Warriors* comics he'd bought second-hand. To his right was his Shakespeare workbook, open so that he could pretend to be studying it if anyone came in. To his left was the computer.

He picked up the workbook, and read from it. "'If it were done, when 'tis done, then 'twere well it were done quickly.' What's that supposed to mean?"

He looked from the book to the computer, then dropped the book and turned on the computer. "If I can't get past level five in three attempts," he said to himself, "then I'll study for an hour."

* * *

Julie was sitting on the garden wall, telling Mairéad her news, when her father arrived home. He dismounted the bike as he reached the driveway, swinging his leg over the huge ladder that was fastened across the frame.

"Hi, Dad! How did it go?"

"Ah, not too bad. This isn't the worst weather to be cleaning windows in." He wheeled the bike along the narrow passage at the far side of the house.

"I'd better go, Mairéad," Julie said. "I'll call for you after dinner."

She followed her father into the backyard. "Mam told me about the holiday," she said.

"So what do you think, love?"

Julie shrugged. "I hope you have a great time."

Her father grinned. "So you're letting us go, then?"

"Only if you promise you'll bring me back something."

"'Course I will, love. Here, hold this a minute."

Julie held the ancient bike steady while her father chained it to the drainpipe.

"Grand. Listen, I was talking to your grandad today. He said you and Brian can stay with him while we're away."

She didn't know how to react. She liked her grandfather, but thought he was a bit odd, living alone like that in such a huge house.

Julie's father noticed her hesitation. "Now, you don't want Brian staying *here*, do you?" He grinned.

She shrugged. "God, no. I wouldn't want any of my friends to meet that stuck-up little pig."

9

She followed her father inside, where he rinsed out his buckets and put them in the press under the sink.

"Your Mam's not here, no?"

Julie shook her head. "She's looking after the Croftons. Betty said she'd give Mam a fiver to mind them for the afternoon. Mam said that anything she can get between now and the holiday was going straight into the post office." Julie looked around the small kitchen. "I suppose I'd better get the dinner started."

"Grand." He paused. "Listen, love. I phoned the Doyles from your grandad's house. Carol said she'd just caught Brian playing games on his computer when he should have been studying. So she was wondering if you could make it longer than two weeks."

Julie looked up at her father. "How long?"

"A month. A week before and a week after the holiday."

She groaned. "Aw, Dad!"

Her father shrugged. "Don't worry, love. Carol said she'll make it worth your while. She said she'll give you two hundred quid for the four weeks, but not to tell Brian or Billy."

Two hundred pounds! Julie said to herself. That would certainly make what would be left of the summer a lot brighter.

She smiled. "Still, four weeks with only Grandad and Brian for company is going to be pretty tough."

"Ah, sure if you're lucky, you might even get to see the ghost."

Julie laughed. "Dad, I'm fifteen! I'm a bit old to be scared by Grandad's ghost stories."

"Well, *he* seems to think the ghost is real enough.

You know, the first time I went back there with Sue – we were only going out about three weeks – your grandad started on about the ghost. Your Mam was mortified, but I thought it was great." He smiled, remembering the scene.

"I think Grandad forgets that we're not five years old any more."

Mr Logan spoke in his vampire accent. "You're never too old to be scared, my child."

Julie laughed: her father's spooky voice always reminded her of the Count from Sesame Street.

"You know, it was only after Sue and I were married that he said I could stop calling him 'Mister Kavanagh', and start calling him 'Tom'." He shrugged. "Your uncle Billy, on the other hand, started calling him 'Tom' from the first day."

Sean set the table while Julie prepared the meal. They chatted as they worked. Despite being an only child, Julie was never lonely.

* * *

It waited.

But something was different. It could sense change. The future told of new arrivals. Young, innocent.

They would come, and they would leave, unknowing, as the others always had. But maybe this time . . . maybe it would be different. They were young – perhaps they could be made to understand.

And with awareness would come fear.

The fear would give it life. It waited for the fear.

CHAPTER TWO

The Saturday marking the start of Julie's stay with her grandfather finally arrived. Julie sat in her bedroom, staring at the pile of books she had to bring with her. I wonder what Brian's weakest at, she asked herself. Maths? English? Geography? Irish? Please God, don't let it be Irish!

Irish had always been her least favourite subject in school, though with perseverance she'd managed to get a C in her Mock Junior Cert, and was hopeful that she'd get at least the same when the results of the actual test came in.

She sighed, then picked up all the books and stuffed them into her holdall. She added a handful of pencils and Biros, and a couple of notebooks.

Julie swung the bag on to her shoulder and groaned under the weight. She met her father on the landing.

"Here," he said, reaching out for the bag, "let me take that."

"Thanks, Dad."

"Ooof!" her father groaned, gripping the bag in his

huge hands. "I didn't know you were bringing your collection of bricks."

Julie followed him down the stairs. "No, they're just books. Most of them are about as interesting as bricks, though."

Mr Logan placed the bag inside the front door, alongside Julie's two other bags, both filled with clothes.

They went into the kitchen. "All set?" Her mother asked. "I've asked Dad to make sure he gets enough food in. Mrs Prentiss calls on Tuesdays, Thursdays and Saturdays, so she'll look after the house. Your grandad still thinks that housework is for women, so don't let him trick you into tidying up after him."

Julie nodded. They had gone over the same things at least ten times a day in the past week.

"If there's any trouble, God forbid, just phone –"

"I know, I know. Just phone Mrs Prentiss and tell her what's happened. Mam, you've told me this thousands of times already."

"Yes, well, if something does happen I want you to know what to do."

"Sorry." Julie turned to her father. "What time is it?"

He squinted at his watch. "Nearly half past. Billy's never late. He has ten seconds."

Mr Logan counted down from ten. As soon as he reached zero, the doorbell rang. He grinned, then walked out to open the door.

Julie looked at her mother. Mrs Logan simply shrugged. "Don't ask me, he always knows."

Julie and her mother listened to the two men pretending to be friends in the hall. They chortled about some inconsequential soccer result, made a few negative remarks about the government, then Julie's father called her.

"Coming!" She walked out into the hall. "Hi, Billy!"

Her uncle smiled warmly. "How's it going, pud?"

"Fine, thanks." She did her best to smile warmly. Her uncle had always imagined that he had a great way with young people, though Julie and her cousins could have told him different.

"So," Billy said, rubbing his hands together, "All ready to go?"

Julie nodded, and began picking up her bags. Billy took them from her, and marched out to the car. "I'll wait for you out here."

Julie kissed her parents. "We'll drop in next week on the way to the airport," Mrs Logan said. "Be good!"

She raced out to the car, waved goodbye to Mairéad who was looking out of her bedroom window, and climbed in.

She hadn't seen Brian in over a year, and almost didn't recognise him. He had grown taller and become more like his father. Brian was wearing a very sour expression. He grunted when Julie said hello, and continued playing with his *Gameboy*.

Julie shook her head in disgust. It was going to be a long four weeks.

* * *

Grandad Tom was waiting at the door when they arrived. "Come in, come in!" He hugged Julie and shook Brian's hand, then turned to Billy. "I'll show my guests to their rooms while you get the bags, Bill."

14

Julie smiled to herself at Billy's look of disgust. Her grandfather had never liked him either.

Grandad Tom was a large, balding man of seventy-two. He always wore old-fashioned, tweedy clothes, and a pair of wire-framed bifocals were permanently perched on the end of his nose.

Julie's room was at the top of the three-storey house. It was small, but neatly arranged. She unpacked her bags and began putting her clothes away. She put her books on top of the dresser, then noticed a fine layer of dust on the surface of the dresser's huge mirror.

Tutting to herself, she took a tissue from her pocket and wiped the dust off. The mirror looked a lot better without the smudges and fingermarks.

When she'd finished putting away her things, she went downstairs to the large living-room in which her grandfather spent most of his time, doing what the family called his "research". Julie had no idea what this meant; he always discussed his research as though she knew what he was talking about, and since they'd spoken of it quite often Julie had reached the stage where she was too embarrassed to admit that she didn't know anything about it.

Grandad Tom was sitting at his desk as Julie entered, He looked up from his book, carefully marked his page with a bookmark, then put it aside and peered over his glasses at his granddaughter. "Well, Julie, what do you think of your room?"

Julie sat down in a big old armchair. "It's great, Grandad. You're very good to let us stay here."

"Not at all. Couldn't have you and Brian killing each other without anyone to mend the cuts and bruises afterwards." He smiled at her, then glanced back at his book.

"Sorry, Grandad," Julie said, "am I interrupting you?"

"Hmm? No, I was just thinking. Do you think the boy will ever manage to catch up with the rest of his class?"

Julie shrugged. "I don't know yet. I'll give him some assessments tonight, see how he's doing."

Her grandfather sighed. "He's a great disappointment to me, you know. Not having any sons myself, I always hoped that Brian would take an interest in the research."

Julie felt herself becoming annoyed. "Why does it have to be a boy? Why can't a *girl* do the research?"

He smiled. "Ah, now don't get upset, young lady. Some things are more suited to men than to women."

"Grandad, this is the twentieth century, not the nineteenth! You can't say things like that!"

He frowned. "Can't I? Why not?"

"Because men and women are created equal. Saying otherwise is just too old-fashioned."

He laughed. "Well, forgive me for being old-fashioned. I can't help it – I'm old! Anyway, let's not get into this particular argument. We were talking about young Brian."

"I don't like him very much," Julie said. "He's conceited, ignorant, rude and spoiled."

Her grandfather nodded. "I agree. But that's just his upbringing. If he was my son I'd soon have that knocked out of him. It's his father's fault, of course. Carol should never have married him. Bill Doyle is far too ambitious for my liking. I think that after your mother got married, Carol just said yes to the first man who proposed." He shook his head sadly. "Bill wanted more than just a wife – he had his eye set on this house. He's just waiting for me to pass on."

Julie was shocked to hear her grandfather speak like that. "I don't think he's *that* bad."

"He is. He always was. The very first thing he did when he came here was check the house out. Bill's father was just the same. Ruthless, conniving. Never could stand the man. In it just for the money, never gave a thought to anyone else . . . despite what your teachers might have you believe, he never intended those plays and sonnets to be classics. It was just his way of making a living."

Julie frowned in puzzlement, thinking that she'd somehow lost track of the conversation along the way, when suddenly the door was pushed open and Brian walked in.

"Come in, my boy!" Tom said, giving Julie a quick wink. "We were just talking about Shakespeare. I believe you're studying him at school?"

Brian sat down. "Yes, we'll be doing *Macbeth*."

Tom nodded. "Ah yes, the Scottish play. I believe that it's considered bad luck to refer to it by name."

Brian grinned. "What, *Macbeth*? What could be bad luck about saying *Macbeth*? *Macbeth* is just a name."

Julie raised her eyes and shook her head. "Brian, that's not funny."

"She's right, Brian. There's a lot of truth in some of those old stories."

"Okay, I promise never to say *Macbeth* again. Oops!"

Grandad Tom sighed. "I presume then that you don't believe in the supernatural, Brian."

"Not in the least," Brian said.

His grandfather sat back in his chair, and looked around the room. "In this age of computers and videos and the rampaging advance of technology, I suppose it's hard to cope with the supernatural." He leaned forward and stared at Brian. "You don't believe in ghosts, then?"

Brian smirked. "Nope."

"You will, Brian. By the end of these four weeks, you *will* believe."

* * *

"You should have seen your face!" Julie laughed. "You went dead white!"

Grandad Tom had gone to bed early after dinner. The setting sun cast an orange glow around the living-room as Julie and Brian prepared a list of subjects Brian would have to study.

Brian looked disgusted. "Stop going on about it."

"Tell me what the theorem of Pythagoras is and I'll stop."

"I don't know it, Julie."

Julie sighed. "You've been reading that page for half an hour, Brian. It's not that hard. In any right-angled triangle, the square on the hypotenuse is equal to the sum of the squares on the other two sides."

Brian stared at the maths book, willing it to become comprehensible. It didn't work. "Right," he said. "First, I do understand it, I just don't believe it. Second, we did this in First Year. Third, I just can't see what use it is."

Julie sucked on the end of her pencil while she

thought about the problem. "All right. Draw a triangle with a right angle in it."

Brian dutifully got out his ruler and did so.

"Now measure the side opposite the right angle. That's the hypotenuse."

"Okay, it's seven point two centimetres."

"And what about the other two sides?"

"Six and four centimetres."

"So the square of six is thirty-six, and the square of four is sixteen. Making fifty-two altogether. What's the square of seven point two?"

Brian reached for his calculator and worked out the sum. "Fifty-one point eight four. See? It doesn't work!"

Julie shook her head. "You have to allow for error, Brian." She grabbed the page and measured the sides. "Look, they're not exactly accurate. Besides, that might not be a right angle. It might be a tenth of a degree off, or something. Trust me, it does work."

One look at Brian's face told her that he still didn't believe it.

"All right. Say you have a right-angled triangle with two sides that are both ten centimetres, okay?"

Brian nodded.

"So what's the combined area of those two sides?"

"Em . . . two hundred."

"So according to the theorem, the hypotenuse has a square of two hundred, right? So the length of the hypotenuse is the square root of two hundred."

Brian fiddled with the calculator. "Fourteen point one four."

"Draw the triangle and measure it."

Brian did so. "It comes out as fourteen point one and a bit."

Julie grinned. "See? I said it works."

"Assuming it does, what use is it?"

"Well, for a start –" Julie paused, and looked up at the ceiling. "I thought he'd gone to bed."

They could hear someone walking across the floor of the room above.

Julie went out to the hall and called softly. "Grandad?"

The footsteps stopped. Brian came out and stood beside her. "Listen," he whispered.

"They've stopped, Brian."

"No, listen!"

The house was completely silent, except for the faint sounds of Grandad Tom snoring gently in the back bedroom.

Julie bit her lip. "There's someone *else* up there!"

Brian looked around, then pulled his grandfather's tightly-rolled umbrella from the stand. "Wait by the phone. If you hear me shouting, ring the police."

He looked up the stairs. Not having any windows, the landing was in darkness. As Brian began to ascend, his own figure blocked out more and more of the light, making the landing even darker.

His heart was thumping madly in his chest. He held the umbrella before him like a club, though he doubted it would be much use against a burglar. He began to wish he'd brought his baseball bat.

Brian walked silently up to the closed door of the front bedroom. He listened carefully, but all he could hear was his grandfather's snoring and his own beating heart. He turned the handle and pushed the door open.

The curtains of the room were drawn, but he could see a shadowy figure standing in the corner. He gasped, and switched on the light.

The figure in the shadows turned into nothing more than an old chair. Otherwise, the room was completely empty. He padded across the thick carpet and looked around the room, then, satisfied with the room's lack of burglars, he went back to the door and switched off the light. He glanced around once more. The shadow in the corner looked exactly like an old chair.

He pulled the door closed and went back down to the living-room.

"Well?" Julie asked. "Everything okay?"

He nodded. "Fine. The room's completely empty, except for a chair in the corner. For a second I thought that it was a person, but I turned the light on."

"Did you check the rest of the room?"

"Yep. Nothing else in there."

"You mean you went in?"

"Of course I went in! I wanted to make sure that no one was hiding."

Julie paused. "Brian . . . I didn't hear you walk across the room."

Brian shrugged. "So? It has a carpet. Why should you?" He stopped. "I see what you mean. Then the footsteps we heard . . ."

"It must have been our imagination, Brian."

Brian nodded, though he wasn't entirely convinced. "I suppose it's time to turn in."

They delayed going to bed for as long as they could, but eventually they packed away their books and made their way up the stairs.

Brian looked at the door to the front bedroom and started to speak, then hesitated. Julie was already unnerved by what they'd heard; it wouldn't do any good to make things worse.

In her bedroom, Julie undressed as quickly as she could and dived under the covers. She lay awake for a long time, but nothing more was heard that night.

Brian also lay awake. What he'd seen had disturbed him much more than the footsteps. As he'd followed Julie up the stairs, he'd seen, through the open door of the front bedroom, a shadowy figure in the corner. It wasn't the chair – he was certain of that. But there was something much worse than that. He shouldn't have been able to see the figure at all.

He clearly remembered closing the door.

* * *

It had almost made contact. The boy – its warped sense of time could also see him as the baby he was and the man he would become – had seen it. He and the girl heard. They were aware.

And with awareness came fear. The fear was very strong, especially in the boy.

Fear lends substance.

CHAPTER THREE

The next day was Sunday, and they'd agreed that Sundays were to be kept as days of rest. When Julie went down to the kitchen for breakfast, she found a note on the table from her grandfather: "Gone to Mass. Going to see some friends after. See you later."

Julie did her best not to think about what had happened the night before. Imagination, that's all it was. Nothing more.

She poured herself a bowl of cornflakes, noting with distaste that Grandad Tom hadn't washed up his own breakfast things.

She finished her breakfast, washed and dried the sinkful of dirty dishes, then went into the living-room. With her grandfather gone, this was Julie's chance to find out exactly what his "research" was all about.

The book he'd been reading yesterday still lay open on the desk. It was a journal of some sort, the pages crammed with Grandad Tom's tiny, neat writing. She turned it over and looked at the cover, but it was blank. She flicked through the pages, but there was nothing obvious to indicate the content.

It didn't appear to be a diary – from what she could make out, it was a collection of theories and explanations concerning the house and the surrounding land, and the lives and deaths of the people who had lived and worked there over the years.

There were no introductions; the text began on the first page. "Built in 1903 by Hubert James Peterson, the house has stood, untouched by fire or any other disaster, ever since. It was bought in 1919 by my father, Ciarán Kavanagh. He had worked with Peterson on the construction, had vowed to buy it, and raise his family here."

Julie read for more than an hour, reaching the mysterious events surrounding the death of her grandfather's baby sister in 1928. She had covered less than a tenth of the book. By the time she finally pushed it away and rubbed her eyes, she understood what Grandad Tom's research was all about: the small portion that she'd read of the book detailed more than a dozen events connected with the ghost.

Out of curiosity, Julie flicked through the book until she came to the entry closest to the day she was born.

"Susan's baby has at last arrived. A girl, whom Susan says she will call Julie, after my mother. My first grandchild! She is beautiful, very like her mother and her aunt were."

Suddenly feeling guilty about reading her grandfather's personal journal, she began to close the book, but stopped when she noticed an entry on the following page.

"Though I myself have neither heard nor seen anything out of the ordinary, Mrs Prentiss claims that yesterday morning she clearly heard someone in the room. She turned, and there was nothing there. Later, she said, she thought she saw the figure of a young woman standing behind her. Of course, I asked how she could see something *behind* her, but she says that she noticed a brief reflection in the mirror. She was unnerved by this, and asked me to remove the mirror from the room. To humour her, I carried it up to the top bedroom. It looks a little out of place on the dresser, but it helps to brighten up the otherwise rather gloomy room."

Julie closed the book. None of the other references to the ghost had mentioned a mirror. She went back upstairs to her room, and stared at the mirror. It did look a little awkward, such a huge mirror on an average three-drawer dresser.

The mirror was again covered in a fine layer of dust. Julie was about to wipe it off, when she noticed the mark. It was vertical, two inches long – as though someone had drawn their finger down the glass, beginning to write in the dust.

As she stared at the mirror, a second mark appeared to the right of the first.

Julie stepped back, shaking her head in disbelief. She reached out behind herself, grabbed for the door handle, and screamed when she touched someone's hand.

* * *

"Sorry!" Brian said. "I'm sorry, I didn't mean to scare you!"

Shaking, Julie said nothing. She simply pointed to the mirror.

25

"What is it? What's the matter?" Brian asked.

"The mirror," Julie stammered. "Look! The writing!"

Brian leaned close to the mirror, and shrugged. "A couple of marks in the dust. So what?"

Still trembling, Julie grabbed her cousin's arm and dragged him out on to the landing. Brian protested as she led him downstairs to the living-room. "What's going on, Julie? Tell me!"

* * *

Julie could see that Brian didn't believe her even as she told him. Even after she showed him the entry in her grandfather's journal, Brian still insisted that she was imagining things.

"Look, Julie, you'd just read about the mirror, and your imagination did the rest."

"It was *not* my imagination!" Julie said. "Brian, yesterday that mirror was covered in dust. I wiped it clean, and you saw it yourself, it's covered in dust again!"

"Okay, if there is a ghost – and I'm not saying that there is – what would it be doing writing on the mirror?"

"How do I know? I'm not an expert." She sighed. "You heard those footsteps last night, didn't you?"

"Yeah. But that could have been anything. The house cooling down, settling. I don't know."

They stopped at the sound of someone coming in through the front door. Grandad Tom stamped his feet and put away his umbrella. "Morning!" He called. "Anyone up yet?"

"We're in here, Grandad!" Julie said.

26

The old man walked into the living-room. "Well, you're up and about early," he said. "I thought you'd still be in –" He paused and looked from one to the other. He nodded slowly, then sat down behind his desk. "So, tell me what you've seen, or heard, or whatever."

* * *

After they'd told him of the events of the previous evening and of that morning, Grandad Tom meticulously wrote it out in his journal. When he'd finally finished, he opened a drawer and took out a huge, yellowing chart, marked off in years and months, and covered in intricate lines. He filled in some more details, then nodded, rolled up the chart and put it back in the drawer.

"What that is," he explained, "is a sort of . . . how would you describe it? It's a map of time, you see, set out from the year 1903, when this house was built, right up to the end of the century. It lists every known sighting of our ghost, and all sorts of things that might be important, like who was in the house, how old they were, and so on. I only hope we find out what it is before we run out of map. I'd hate to have to draw that out again."

"A map of time . . ." Julie said thoughtfully. "Why not call it a diary?"

Grandad Tom looked surprised. "A diary? Well, yes, I suppose that's what it is. It never occurred to me before."

"I presume you're looking for a pattern in the sightings," Brian said. "A computer could do that for you, if you programmed it to."

27

"Yes, but could *you* program it?" Grandad Tom asked. "I know I couldn't."

"Do you have any theories about the ghost, Grandad?" Julie asked.

He nodded. "Yes, yes I do. You know the stories about banshees, don't you? The sighting of the banshee is supposed to warn of a death, either your own or someone close to you. If you take that at its most basic level, all we really have is the sighting of a banshee, and a death. There's no connection, but if a death occurs every time a banshee is seen, what does that tell us?"

"The banshee knows when someone will die," Brian said.

"Or," said Julie, "the banshee causes the death."

Grandad Tom agreed that either could be right. "Of course, look at it this way – if someone sees a strange woman dressed in white, and no one dies, nobody will ever think it's a banshee. Similarly, if someone dies, and no one has seen a banshee, nothing is said. Do you get my point?"

Julie nodded, but Brian shook his head. "No, I don't get it."

Julie turned to him. "A banshee isn't a spirit that warns of death, it's only the *belief* in a spirit that warns of death. You have to have the death *and* the sighting of the woman in white to make it into a banshee."

"Ah," Brian said. "Now I'm with you. So what's that got to do with our ghost?"

"Our ghost, as you so correctly put it, always seems to appear around the time of great emotional trauma. Specifically, births and deaths."

Brian laughed. "I can just about believe that a ghost

28

can cause a death, but I'll never believe that it can cause a birth!"

"That's *not* what I mean," Grandad Tom said sourly. "The ghost is always here, it's just when we're more emotional that we become aware of it. People are particularly emotional when someone dies or a child is born."

Julie began to feel cold. In her mind she repeatedly ran over the question that no one dared to ask out loud. We're only aware of it when we're emotional. And we're emotional when someone is born, or when someone dies . . . so why is it here now?

She looked at her grandfather. Is *he* going to die?

29

CHAPTER FOUR

"You know," Brian said, "the more I think about it, the more it seems like we were all imagining things."

Julie looked up from her book. "Huh? What are you talking about?"

"The ghost. What we saw, what we heard." He shrugged. "I don't know, it's like something we saw in a film. It doesn't seem real."

It had been six days since their talk with Grandad Tom, and there had been no more footsteps, no more sightings. Even the mirror in Julie's bedroom had remained free of dust and marks.

It was Saturday, lunch-time. Julie and Brian were sitting on the front porch, taking a break from their studies. Brian had been progressing well. Without the distractions of school and his various electronic toys, he'd found that studying became, if not exactly interesting, then at least tolerable.

Julie, too, had found the week away from home quite refreshing. She was faced with none of the housework that she'd had to do at home as Mrs Prentiss, the middle-aged woman who looked after Grandad Tom, was more than efficient at keeping the house clean and tidy.

Without a television to distract them, Julie and Brian found themselves raiding their grandfather's library for reading material, with the result that Brian's grasp of the English language had improved dramatically. He could barely believe it himself – he'd read three books in a week, over eight hundred pages. One of the books was *Lord of the Flies*: Brian had thoroughly enjoyed the book and was astonished to learn that it was on the reading list for the Leaving Cert. "How can they approve something so violent?" he'd asked Julie.

Julie had smiled, and said that by the time the Leaving came around, he'd have read and analysed the book a dozen times. By then, it might not seem so enjoyable.

That morning, they'd studied *Macbeth*. Though Brian still insisted on referring to the play by name every chance he could, he had gained some respect for Shakespeare. What had seemed meaningless ramblings transformed themselves into beautiful, carefully-crafted prose, and Brian strained to learn the important soliloquies by heart. He was particularly taken with the character of Lady Macbeth, whom he'd subsequently dubbed "Macbetty".

As they sat in the porch, munching their way through the sandwiches that Mrs Prentiss had made for them, and waiting for their parents to drop by on the way to the airport, Brian read from the book. "'Is this a dagger which I see before me, the handle towards my hand? Come, let me clutch thee: I have thee not, and yet I see thee still . . .' The first mention of holograms in literature," he laughed.

31

Julie smiled. "Oscar Wilde said that the difference between literature and fiction is that fiction isn't worth reading and literature is never read. At least I *think* it was Oscar Wilde. It might have been Mark Twain."

"Oscar Wilde also said 'Please don't lock me up, I'll never do it again', so what does he know?" Brian flicked through the book again. "'Double, double, toil and trouble; Fire burn and cauldron bubble.' So this is where that comes from."

"Where did you think it came from? Darina Allen?" Brian grinned.

"You should read the notes, Brian. They explain a lot of the confusing stuff."

"You know, this thing is full of quotes. Look, 'Something wicked this way comes.' I saw that film. That guy was in it, you know, the guy who was in *Brazil*. Jonathan Pryce."

"Somehow, I don't think that's entirely relevant to Shakespeare. Or your exams, for that matter." Julie grabbed Brian's wrist and looked at his watch. "They should have been here by now. Do you mind not going to Spain?"

Brian shrugged. "I did, but not now. I mean, despite all this torture and not having a telly, I'm having a good time."

Julie smiled. "Me too."

"I miss my computer, though," Brian said.

"Don't you have any *real* friends?"

"Sure I do. Loads of them."

"So what do you normally do together?"

"We swap software. Play games. Try to copy protected software."

"Brian, that's the same as stealing."

He laughed. "So is taping songs from the radio, and you do that."

"That's completely different. I only tape songs I can't afford to buy."

"Yeah, but the average computer game costs nearly fifty quid. I can't afford to buy *them*."

"I thought you lot were well off. You must be, with a villa in Spain."

"That's not really ours," Brian said. "We just time-share it."

"Still, it's a lot more than we have. And you have a video, and *two* cars."

Brian sighed. "I don't understand what Grandad has against my dad," he said. "I mean, he's successful, intelligent, got a brilliant son . . ."

Julie grinned. "You must mean Keith. It can't be you – if you're so brilliant how come you're so far behind in school?"

"Very funny. Anyway, it's well-known that lots of brilliant people did badly in school, like Einstein. I read a book about him once. Well, I read most of it."

"I don't think it works as easily as that. If it did, we'd be up to our necks in geniuses."

They heard a car coming up the long drive. "Here they are!" Julie said. She stood up and waved.

The car came to a stop in front of the porch. Carol Doyle and Susan Logan were sitting in the back, with Brian's sister Gemma between them. Seeing them like that, Julie was surprised how alike the three were; Gemma looking like a nine-year-old version of the twins. Of course, Julie realised, I'm just like them myself. Brian's brother, Keith, was sitting on his mother's lap.

They climbed out of the car, greeted Julie and Brian and stretched a little.

Julie hugged her parents. "Are you having a good time?" her father asked.

"Great! We've gotten a lot of work done."

Billy ruffled his son's hair. "So it's going well, son? That Shakespeare? Let's hear some."

Brian shrugged, and put down the book. He cleared his throat, and spoke in what he liked to think of as his Shakespeare accent. "If it were done when 'tis done, then 'twere well It were done quickly: if the assassination Could trammel up the consequence, and catch With his surcease success; that but this blow Might be the be-all and the end-all, here, But here, upon this bank and shoal of time, We'd jump the life to come."

His mother smiled at him. "Now that's some improvement. But do you know what it *means*?"

Brian nodded. "Sure. 'If it were done when 'tis done', means 'If it was over, when the deed was done.'"

Seán Logan put his arm around Julie's shoulder and let her lead him into the house. "So, any sign of . . ." he paused and rolled his eyes for dramatic effect. ". . . the ghost?"

Julie glanced at Brian, then back to her father. "No, nothing. You didn't really expect there to be, did you?"

He laughed. "Ah, now, your Mam gave out to me for mentioning it in the first place. I just had to be sure your imagination hadn't gone wild."

Mrs Logan playfully thumped her husband on the arm. "Seán, I'm warning you!"

Brian's mother looked around the living-room and kitchen. "Dad's not here, then?"

Brian shook his head. "He's gone fishing. I said that he'd miss you, but he laughed and said that he was sure he'd remember what you all looked like."

Billy laughed. "And how is he then, keeping well?"

Julie looked at him. Was Billy really waiting for him to drop dead, as Grandad Tom had said? "He's fine," she said. "Never been fitter, in fact."

Brian took Gemma and Keith to look around the house, while Julie's Dad and her uncle Billy went back out to the car to make a quick check on the engine. Billy said that they'd had a bit of trouble with the brakes, and had been forced to stop at a garage, which was why they'd been late; something that Seán seemed rather pleased about.

Carol and Susan spent half an hour wandering through the house with Julie, telling her about their childhood. "We used to pretend to be each other," Carol said. "It never fooled Dad, but we gave Mrs Prentiss a terrible time."

"How long has she been working here?" Julie asked.

"Twenty years, or something," her mother said. "She was here the night you were born, love. Dad was so nervous he couldn't do anything, so she stayed over to look after him. You know, she knew the minute you were born, she says. She was asleep in a chair in the front bedroom, and she dreamt that I was right behind her. She woke up, then phoned the hospital. Not five minutes after you were born."

Julie felt herself growing cold. She remembered the passage in her grandfather's journal.

* * *

They left shortly afterwards, with a promise of presents and a cheery wave out the car window. Brian and Julie stood on the porch and watched them go.

"That was creepy, what Mam said about Mrs Prentiss," Julie said.

"Don't talk about it. You're only making things worse."

She shivered. "I wish Grandad was here."

"Me too."

Julie went back into the hall. "I'll be down in a minute," she said.

She climbed the stairs to the first landing. The door to the front bedroom was closed. She turned the handle and pushed the door open. The curtains were drawn, and the room was empty, except for the chair that Brian had spoken of.

She walked to the window, pulled open the curtains and looked out at the view. She heard Brian come in behind her. "It's not a bad view," she said. "It's really a shame that no one uses this room."

She peered out. "Look! You can see the river from here! We should go for a swim later on, what do you think?"

Brian didn't answer. She turned around to ask him again.

There was no one there.

* * *

Julie paused. She was sure that she'd heard him behind her. She remembered hearing his breathing, the shuffling of his feet on the carpet as he moved forward to look over her shoulder.

But there was no one there.

Julie blessed herself, and said the Our Father. Then, somehow finding the strength and courage to move, she walked straight out of the room, and ran up to her bedroom. She sat on the bed, shaking and crying. "Oh God, oh God! Please make it stop! Make it go away!"

Eventually she managed to regain control of herself. She took a few deep breaths, then dried her eyes on her handkerchief. She sniffed a little, then laughed at the way she'd panicked over nothing. You big baby, she said to herself. Mustn't let Brian know I've been crying. She blew her nose, then stood up and examined her face in the mirror. Not too bad, a little puffy round the eyes. Best to wait for a few minutes.

Then she noticed that she had to squint at her reflection to see past the dust. She jumped back. Written in the dust was a single letter. The eighth letter of the alphabet. H.

* * *

The screaming stopped. It was confused. Had it heard the screaming, or imagined it? Or had it been screaming itself?

The girl had brought it forward, up, out of the timeless darkness. The girl had unwittingly called it. This time there was hope. The girl's love for her family was very strong. Somehow that love had pulled it into the real world, though only for a few brief seconds.

It knew that it needed this girl. Without her, it was damned forever. But this girl had within her the power to understand, the power to believe.

That was what fed it most. Belief.

CHAPTER FIVE

"Will you have another one, Tom?" the young barman asked.

Tom looked at his empty pint glass, started to nod, then stopped and said "No, I'd better not, Davey. The young 'uns will smell the drink off me."

"Ah, sure you've only had the one." He picked up a glass and began polishing it.

Tom fixed the barman with his gaze. "Davey, how old do you think I am?"

Davey looked at him and shrugged. "I don't know . . . sixty?"

Tom laughed. "I'm seventy-two. And do you know how I managed to stay so young-looking?"

"Tell us," Davey said, taking up Tom's glass and wiping the bar with a damp cloth.

"I managed to stay so young-looking by knowing when it was time to go home." He pushed himself off the bar stool, picked up his fishing gear, and walked towards the door. "Goodnight, Davey."

"'Night, Mr Kavanagh."

The door swung open just as Tom was reaching for the handle. A man about Tom's age walked in.

"Tom! How's the man?"

"Grand, Joe. Yourself?"

"Can't complain." Joe glanced at Tom's bag and fishing rod. "Catch anything?"

"Just the one," Tom said. He put the gear down and held his right hand about six inches above his left. "And it had the most peculiar black body with a white head," he grinned.

Joe grinned back. "Sure, I was doing a bit of fishing myself today."

Tom frowned. "I didn't see you there."

"I was down by the shores."

"What shores?"

Joe smiled and rubbed his hands together. "Mine's a pint, thanks very much."

Tom shook his head and laughed. "G'way out of that, you devious git!"

Joe grabbed Tom's sleeve and began to pull him towards the bar. "Come on, Tom, you probably owe me a brewery by now."

Tom picked up his gear and walked back to the bar. "Never! You're the man who's conned every man in town out of a pint. No one owes you anything."

"That's a cruel thing to say, Tom. Buy me a pint so I can cry into it."

They sat at the bar and ordered a couple of pints, laughing as they talked over old times.

* * *

"He's been gone ages," Julie said. "I hope he's all right."

"What'll we do if he doesn't come home?" Brian asked.

"Mam said that if anything happens to ring Mrs Prentiss."

Brian nodded, and looked at his watch. "It's just gone seven. If he's not back by ten we'll ring her."

They were sitting in the living-room. They had the radio on, but neither was paying much attention to it. Julie had told Brian what had happened in the front bedroom, and in her own bedroom at the top of the house, but when Brian had examined the mirror all they could see were a few vague marks.

Brian was reading through his grandfather's huge dictionary. Julie had accused him of looking up the rude words, but Brian had insisted that all he was doing was trying to pass the time.

He looked up at Julie, who was sitting at the desk. "What are you doing?"

"I'm writing."

"I can see that. What is it?"

"A letter."

"Oh," Brian said. "To your boyfriend, is it?"

Julie scowled at him. "No, to my friend Mairéad. I don't have a boyfriend."

"Why not? Are you afraid of men, or something?"

Julie was shocked. "What sort of a question is that?"

Brian shrugged. "Some women are afraid of men, that's why they don't go out with anyone."

"Where do you hear such things?"

"From Dad. He knows a lot about women."

Julie threw her pen down and folded her arms. "Is

that so? I suppose he *told* you he knew a lot about women."

"He did, as a matter of fact."

"Did it ever occur to you that he might just be boasting? Honest to God, I don't know what your mother ever saw in him."

It was Brian's turn to be shocked. "What do you mean? What are you saying about my dad?"

Julie swallowed. She felt like a fool. Inwardly, she sighed. It was all out in the open now, might as well carry on. "He's rude, and mean, and self-centred, for a start."

Brian was raging. "No! You're wrong! When has he ever been rude to *you*? Or mean? Or anything but nice?"

Oh, well done, Julie! she said to herself. Better stop this now. "I'm sorry, Brian. I didn't mean it. I'm just tired and upset, that's all."

Brian nodded. "Okay, okay. I understand."

In the corner, the portable radio continued talking to itself, announcing songs and playing dedications. They sat silently. Julie went back to her letter and Brian to his book, both deliberately not looking at the other, neither knowing what to say.

* * *

"Brian," Julie whispered.

He was lying half asleep on the couch. "Yeah?"

"Brian!"

"What?"

"There's something in here."

Brian sat up with a start. "What! Where?" He looked around the room, but could see nothing.

Julie stared at him, her eyes wide with fright. "Can't you hear it?"

Brian hesitated. He listened carefully, then shook his head. "No. Nothing."

"Sort of a hiss, and voices, very faint."

Brian sat still, barely moving, not even breathing. "You're right," he whispered. He stood up, and slowly walked around the room, trying to place the source of the sound.

Brian stopped and turned to Julie. "I know what it is," he said. "I can hear the voices clearly."

Julie stared at him. "What are they saying?"

He frowned, then turned back to her. "They're saying . . . it's kind of fuzzy, but it sounds like . . . no. That can't be right. That can't be true." His eyes widened in panic. "No! It can't be! It can't be! It's too horrible!"

Julie began to shake. "What? Brian! What is it? What are they saying?"

"They're saying . . ." He stared at her, and gulped. "They're saying that Madonna has a new album in the charts."

Julie paused. *"What?"*

Brian grinned, and pointed to the corner of the room. "It's just the radio, Julie. The batteries must be running down."

She collapsed back into her chair. "You dirty . . . you practically scared me to death!"

Brian fell around the room laughing. "That'll teach you to not to say bad things about people you don't really know!" There were tears in his eyes, and he had to grab on to the mantelpiece to hold himself up.

* * *

The girl's fear, then her anger at being tricked, did not go to waste.

It was feeding well from her emotions. It was forming a strong bond with this time, it was gaining more and more control over itself and would soon be able to manipulate the real world.

But still it did not know what it was, and it yearned to know, it needed to know. Identity was what gave individuals their power, and soon it would need that power.

It would need much power, if it was to be able to bring about change . . .

The children were tired, emotionally and physically. It knew they would be susceptible, but it decided to wait; affecting the real world used so much of its energy — best to wait, and rest, and watch.

* * *

"Is it a dog?" Julie asked.

Brian shook his head. "Nope. That's nineteen. One more."

Julie raised her eyes. "I don't know . . . you're a bloody cheat anyway. I *did* get that last one. A chair was the right answer."

"No. It was a *picture* of a chair. Entirely different."

"I still think that's cheating."

Brian just smiled at her. "Come on, one more question, then it'll be ten-nil."

She leaned back in the chair and stared at the ceiling.

Ten-nil! Brian was going to be insufferable! She thought back over the clues. It *had* to be a dog! After the argument over the chair, Julie had made certain to ask whether the object was a picture of anything. So it had to be a dog, and there was no way he could cheat this time, unless . . .

Julie grinned at him. "I know! Is it two dogs?"

Brian looked away in disgust. "How did you know that?"

"I knew you'd find a way to cheat somehow."

"All right then, it's nine-one. You'll never catch up, anyway. You think of one."

"Okay." Julie looked around the room, then realised that he was watching to see what she looked at. She closed her eyes and tried to visualise something that Brian would never guess. She opened her eyes and smiled. "I've got one."

"Is it animal, vegetable, or mineral?"

"Mineral," Julie said.

He looked her straight in the eye. "Is it a desk?"

She stared back at him. This is impossible, she said to herself, he's reading my mind! She was about to answer when they heard someone opening the front door.

Grandad Tom entered the room, looking a little red around the cheeks and grinning wider than usual. "I'm drunk," he announced. "And I don't care."

"You will in the morning, Grandad," Brian said.

He grunted and flopped down into his favourite armchair. "So what have you two been up to?"

"Aside from worrying about you," Julie said. "We've been playing twenty questions."

44

"Ah! Who's turn is it now?"

"Mine," Julie said.

"Is it a desk?" the old man asked.

Julie's mouth dropped open. "What is this? Is everyone but me able to read minds?"

Brian laughed. "So it *is* a desk! Yes! Ten-one! I am the champion!"

Grandad Tom looked at Julie and winked. "Don't worry about it, dear. The desk is the biggest thing in the room. When I was young we used to play the same sort of game, and the answer was almost always a desk."

Julie shook her head and laughed.

"Now, to bed, both of you," their grandfather said.

Julie and Brian began packing away their things. "What about you, Grandad?" Brian asked.

"Never mind me, I'll sleep where I am. I'm used to it. Would one of you get the quilt off my bed?"

Brian raced upstairs and came back with the huge old quilt. He took his grandfather's shoes off and wrapped the quilt around him. His eyes were closing and he was almost asleep already.

Julie kissed him on the forehead. "Goodnight," she said.

He yawned and smacked his lips. "Goodnight, Susan."

They switched off the light and closed the door behind them. "Goodnight, Susan!" Brian whispered.

"Very funny!" Julie said.

Julie made her way up to her room. She opened the door, switched on the light and looked at the mirror. There was a fine coating of dust, but no marks in it. She undressed quickly, slipped on her nightdress, then switched off the light and climbed into bed.

She lay awake for a while, wondering how her parents were getting on with the Doyles, then she fell into a deep, peaceful sleep.

* * *

Brian sat up in bed for nearly an hour, playing Tetris on his *Gameboy*. His eyes felt heavy, but still he could not stop playing. He found himself drifting off, and when he looked back at the machine the screen was blank. He frowned at it. He didn't remember turning it off. Then, as he watched, a short black vertical line of pixels appeared. Then another, to the right of the first. A third line appeared, horizontally crossing the first two.

Brian stared at the machine. He couldn't believe what he was seeing. As the fourth line began to appear, Brian switched off the machine and dropped it on to the duvet. Then he opened the back and pulled out the batteries.

He sat unmoving in the bed and didn't fall asleep for a long, long time.

CHAPTER SIX

Julie woke early, in plenty of time for Mass, and went downstairs to discover that her grandfather had, at some stage during the night, gone upstairs to sleep in his bed.

She boiled the kettle and made a pot of tea, then went up to wake Grandad Tom. "Grandad? Are you going to Mass?"

He mumbled an answer. Julie shook him harder. "Grandad. You'll be late."

He didn't move. "Grandad, if you get up now I'll make your breakfast."

This time he opened his eyes and sat up. "That's a good girl! Get us a glass of water, would you?"

Julie brought him his water and went up to Brian's room. She knocked on the door. "Brian?"

There was no answer. She opened the door and peered in. Brian was sitting up, though fast asleep. Julie noticed that the light was still on, and his pocket-sized game computer was lying on the bed. She sighed, switched off the light and closed the door behind her. Brian could always get the twelve o'clock service, anyway.

* * *

Julie walked to Mass with Grandad Tom. It seemed that the old man knew everyone they passed. Five people stopped to offer them a lift, but Grandad Tom declined them all, saying that the walk to church was a sacrifice he made to God.

Julie asked him about this, but he just grinned and said that he couldn't stand cars; most people drove too fast.

The small church was less than half full. The young priest charged through the service, and finished with some announcements regarding the parish's upcoming summer festival. Julie hardly noticed any of it – the priest's sermon had been about cleansing the soul and casting out evil. It set Julie thinking.

On the way home, Julie asked her grandfather if anyone had ever tried to have the ghost exorcised.

Grandad Tom laughed. "No, never. I don't really hold with all that sort of thing. I mean, there *is* a ghost, all right, but they say that exorcism can be very dangerous. No, our ghost does no harm. We'll let it be. Besides, I'd hate to get rid of the thing and never find out what it was."

"But it's dangerous, Grandad. I mean, someone could die of fright. I nearly did," Julie said.

He stopped, and pointed at a nearby tree with his umbrella. "Look at that tree, Julie. What is it?"

"It's a sycamore."

"And being a sycamore it's deciduous, right? Every autumn that tree loses its leaves. They blow across the road and build up into huge piles at that hedge. A sudden gust of wind might blow one of those piles of leaves into an oncoming car and cause the driver to crash."

"That's not very likely," Julie said.

Grandad Tom continued walking. "Not likely, but you do admit it's possible. Now, should that tree be cut down?"

"Well, no. It's not likely enough to cause any damage, and it wouldn't be fair to ruin such a good tree."

"So does that answer your question about the ghost?"

Julie looked at him. "To be honest, no."

"The ghost doesn't do any harm. It's there, we're there. There's room for all of us."

"Do you know what it is, Grandad?"

He looked at her, began to nod, and then said "No. I used to think it was the ghost of my mother, but there were sightings long before she died."

"Sightings? You mean someone has actually *seen* the ghost?"

"Not really sightings. What Brian said he saw last week was about as much as anyone has ever seen. A figure in the dark. I've never seen anything like that myself, but I've heard a few strange sounds, and often I've felt that there was something in the room with me."

"Yesterday, when you were out, I was in the front bedroom, the one above the living-room. I was looking out the window, and I heard Brian come in behind me. I was talking to him, I knew he was there, but when I looked around no one was there."

"You should have told me this last night," her grandfather said.

"You weren't in the best of form last night, Grandad."

49

"This is true. Did anything else happen?"

"There was some more writing on the mirror. The letter 'H'."

Grandad Tom was silent for a while. "You know, this is the most important thing that's ever happened regarding the ghost. It's trying to make contact. I wonder . . ." He looked at her. "Julie, it all seems to be revolving around you. You know you're named after my mother?"

Julie nodded.

"If it *is* her ghost, she might have formed a bond with you. I don't know. Like I said, the ghost has been around for a long time."

"Am I like her?" Julie asked.

"Oh yes, very like her. All the women in the family always have been. Your mother, her sister, even little Gemma. All very alike."

"But has the ghost ever contacted any of them?"

He shook his head. "Not that I know of."

Julie was getting worried. "Then why me?"

"I don't know. It could be just coincidence."

They walked the rest of the way in silence. Julie wondered what bond she could possibly have with a ghost that had haunted the house for ninety years.

* * *

In the vestry, the altar boys were chatting about videos. Father McCanney, the priest who'd given the Mass, listened to the boys as he disrobed. He shook his head sadly. Didn't they listen to a single word I said out there? he wondered. I only hope my sermon didn't go over everyone else's heads the same way.

There was a knock on the door, and Father Robert Mitchell, the parish priest, entered. "Nice sermon, Peter. A bit *too* heavy on the fires of Hell, but otherwise I think you woke a few of them up."

Father McCanney grinned. "Thanks, Robert." He nodded to the altar boys. "It doesn't seem to have affected some people, though."

"All right, boys," Father Mitchell said, "change and get on home. Well done." He returned his attention to Father McCanney. "Still looking for a purpose?"

The young priest shrugged. "I suppose so." He sighed. "What's wrong with the world today? Real good and evil are very rare. It's like everything else is in shades of grey. How can you tell people not to sin when it seems that everyone around them is sinning far more than they are?"

The older priest patted him on the shoulder, and smiled. "Don't let that worry you. People are inherently good, they just stray from the path from time to time. We're only here to guide them, not to judge them."

Father McCanney rolled up his vestments and stuffed them in a plastic carrier bag. "We have to be here for more than that, Robert. I believe each of us has been chosen for a special reason. If we were only here to guide people, why have we heard the calling? No, there's something out there, some great work I've been chosen to do."

Father Mitchell laughed. "You should have become a missionary, Peter."

The younger priest looked at him seriously. "There *is* something out there for me, and I intend to find it."

"Be careful, my son. It may find *you*."

* * *

It watched the boy as he wandered through the house. The previous night, it had crept into his imagination as he had slept, and shaped his dreams.

But the boy had been too frightened, and even though it had needed his fear, the boy had somehow shut it out. He had managed to bring logic to his dream.

But now he was alone. It would try again.

* * *

Brian drifted from room to room. He was exhausted, having lain awake for hours the night before. When he woke, he'd noticed that the batteries were still in his *Gameboy*. So it *must* have been a dream, he told himself. Even in my dream I knew that the *Gameboy* wouldn't work without batteries.

He wondered how long Julie and Grandad Tom would be. Their note had said they were at Mass, but hadn't mentioned what time they expected to be home. Eventually, Brian got bored waiting, and went out into the huge back garden.

The garden was cluttered with plastic gnomes and small white wooden blocks with short poles in them. Brian had always wondered what those things were for. He made a mental note to ask his grandfather.

There was a large oak at the back of the garden. Brian remembered that there had been a swing attached to it when he was a child. All that was left was a ragged six-inch length of rope tied to one of the branches. He looked up, and saw that the tattered skeleton of his old kite was still entangled in the tree's branches. He smiled, remembering his father trying to climb up and retrieve the kite. Brian had cried all the way home, and had only stopped when his father promised him a new kite.

Maybe I *was* a bit spoiled, Brian said to himself. He looked up at the tree. The kite didn't seem too far up. He jumped up and grabbed hold of the first thick branch and pulled himself up on to it. Holding on to a couple of smaller branches, Brian manoeuvred himself around the tree until he could see the kite. It was about ten feet above his head.

Brian climbed on to the next branch, but couldn't go any further while holding on to the trunk. He crawled along the branch, to where it forked, and looked up. There was a much sturdier branch above him. He stood up, being careful not to over balance, and reached up. No good, it was just a tiny bit too high.

He looked at the kite. It was only three feet away now. Brian made a decision. He jumped and caught the branch above. It gave a little under his weight, but was strong enough to hold him. Wrapping his legs around the branch, he was able to reach out and grab the kite.

He grinned to himself. After all these years, he finally had his kite back. He looked down. The ground seemed a long way off. He edged his way out along the branch, until it had sagged enough for him to drop to the lower one. He couldn't climb any lower with the kite in his hand, so he threw it to the ground.

Brian glanced back at the house, and froze. There was a shadowy figure watching him from the kitchen window.

* * *

Grandad Tom opened the hall door, and Julie followed him inside.

"Brian?" Julie called. There was no reply. "He must be gone to Mass," Julie said.

Grandad Tom took off his jacket and hung it on the coat stand, then put away his umbrella. "Put the kettle on, love, I'm going up to get my slippers," he called as he made his way up the stairs.

Julie opened the kitchen door, and walked in. She picked up the kettle, removed the lid, and was filling the kettle at the sink when she looked out to the window and saw Brian lying on the ground, under the giant oak tree.

* * *

"He's just had the wind knocked out of him," Doctor Mellery said. "He'll be fine. Let him rest for a few days."

Between the three of them, they managed to carry Brian into the living-room, and place him on the sofa. He was groaning softly, and badly bruised, but there were no bones broken.

"You were right not to move him before you called me; that's the first thing most people try to do, and it can be dangerous," the doctor said. "I've given him a couple of pain-killers. They're pretty strong, so he'll be numb for a few hours." He quickly scribbled out a prescription, and handed it to Julie. "Take this to the chemist first thing in the morning."

Julie nodded, and slipped the prescription into the pocket of her jeans.

"Is there anything we can do for him now?" Grandad Tom asked.

The doctor shook his head. "No, just let him be. I don't know, a lad of his age should know better than to be climbing around trees." He picked up his bag, then fished in his pocket and handed her his card. "Give me a ring if there's any problem."

Julie thanked him, and sat with Brian as her grandfather saw the doctor to the door.

* * *

Brian was unconscious for nearly an hour, and when he did finally waken, he was confused and couldn't remember where he was.

He drifted in and out of sleep for the rest of the afternoon. Julie sat beside him, reading and listening to the radio. Grandad Tom had gone out, leaving strict instructions that Julie was to phone Mrs Prentiss if anything happened.

Brian's watch beeped, and Julie looked up from her book to see him awake, and staring at her.

"Julie?" His voice was coarse and weak.

"It's okay, Brian. The doctor said you'll be fine."

"Julie, I saw it again. I saw the ghost."

Julie's book slipped out of her hands and thudded to the floor. "Where?"

"I was in the tree, getting down. I looked at the kitchen window, and it was there." He tried to sit up, but the pain from his bruised ribs was too much.

Despite her fear, Julie wanted to know. "What did it look like, Brian?"

He stared at her. "You. I thought it was you. And as I watched, it seemed to change into an old woman, then into Gemma, then into my mother. Or *your* mother," he added.

"Did it do anything? How long was it there?"

He shrugged. "I don't know. It seemed like I was watching it for years. It didn't do anything, it just stood there." He hesitated. "I couldn't really see it clearly, but . . . it seemed to be screaming."

CHAPTER SEVEN

Julie didn't know what to say. She simply sat there, staring at Brian.

He could see the horror in Julie's eyes and tried to think of something to console her. "Maybe I didn't see anything," he said. "Maybe when I hit my head I just dreamed it."

"No," Julie said. "No. You saw it. It's real."

"Last night, I was playing with my *Gameboy*. I was half asleep, and I kept dozing off. At one stage I woke up and saw that the screen was blank. I thought it was broken at first, but as I watched the letter 'H' appeared. I was scared. I turned it off and pulled out the batteries. When I woke up this morning, the batteries were still in it. I thought it must have been a dream."

"Before I went to Mass this morning, I checked on you. You were asleep sitting up, and the light was on."

Brian took a deep breath, "Julie, it's trying to make contact. Go upstairs and check your mirror. See if there's anything there."

She shook her head. "No! If there *is* anything, I don't want to know!"

"Julie, you have to. We have to find out what it is."

"You're wrong! We don't *have* to do anything. Anyway, I think I know what it is. Grandad said that he used to think it was the ghost of his mother."

"The ghost has been around since long before his mother died," Brian said.

"So he says, but what if he's wrong? What if the early appearances of the ghost were something else?"

"I'll tell you what, have a look at Grandad's chart and see how many women have died here. It has to be one of them, right?"

"I suppose so." Julie opened the drawer in her grandfather's desk and took out the chart. She unrolled it on the desk, and placed paperweights on the corners to stop it from rolling back.

Julie read through the chart as well as she could, and compiled a list of those who had died in the house. She put away the chart and sat back down beside Brian. "Okay, in 1928 Grandad's sister, Gwendolyn Kavanagh, died. She was only three, the poor thing. In 1936 his father, Ciarán, died, then his mother in 1943. In 1973, his wife died. Our grandmother. She was only forty-seven." Julie felt sad for her grandfather. He'd lost so many people in his life.

"That's the lot?" Brian asked.

Julie arched her eyebrow. "Isn't it enough?"

He smiled. "I didn't mean that the way it sounded, Julie."

"I know."

"Well, assuming the ghost *is* female – and it certainly looks female – we can cross our great-grandad off the list, leaving three."

"Leaving two," Julie corrected. She stood up and took a picture from the mantelpiece. "Look, this is our grandmother. You said that the ghost looked like me, or Mam, or Carol, or Gemma, right? So if it looked like Granny as well, then it wouldn't look like Grandad's mother, would it?" She showed him the picture.

"No, that's not her."

"So if we get our looks from Grandad's mother, then it must be her, right?"

"That's a good point," Brian said. "And Grandad's sister was only three. I guess we can rule her out too. Ghosts stay behind because of some unfinished business, or so I've heard. They can't pass on to the next world until they've accomplished one final task on earth. There can't be many unfinished tasks that a three-year-old would leave behind. I don't imagine an unfinished jigsaw would be important enough. Besides, I definitely saw the ghost as an older woman."

Despite being scared, Julie felt excited at having come so far to solving the problem. "More to the point, there was writing on the mirror. Would a three-year-old be able to write? So that leaves Grandad's mother, Julie Kavanagh."

Brian looked thoughtful for a moment. "I wonder how she died," he said. "Maybe she was murdered, or something."

"Brian! How could you say such a thing?"

He shrugged. "You never can tell. Murder has been known to happen."

Julie glared at him, but he just smiled back. "Look, Julie. If something like that did happen, maybe by finding the killer we can release her spirit. Or if it was something else, maybe we can help in some way."

"Aren't you scared by all this?" Julie asked.

"Yes, but now that I've seen it, now that we know what it is, I feel a lot better about it."

"We'd better not say anything about this to Grandad."

"You're right," Brian said. Then he grinned. "After all, he might be the killer."

Julie picked up a cushion and threw it at him. "That is a rotten thing to say!"

"Ouch! Stop!" Brian laughed. "I'm a sick man, remember!"

"You'll be a dead man, Doyle!"

"Aha! So, maybe murder *does* run in the family!"

Julie couldn't think of any way to respond, so she stuck her tongue out at him.

* * *

It lost contact with the human world and drifted once more.

We are our past, it said to itself. That is what shapes us, what gives us meaning. My past seems forever out of reach; when I grasp at a memory, it fades. But I am getting stronger. The girl's memory is like an open book to me, yet it is as though it is written in a language I only barely understand. Unlike her, I do not remember, I only experience . . .

Soon, as it so often did, it revisited the time of its death, when it had been severed from its mortal body and left to wander between the worlds of the living and the dead.

It tried to concentrate on what it was seeing, but the

images floated and faded before it could comprehend them, the words forgotten as soon as they were heard.

But this time was different. A face appeared, clear and certain. The old man. The children's grandfather. His face was young, then old, then young again, continually changing. But his eyes were constant. They were filled with sorrow and tears. The tears rolled down his cheeks, and as the image faded into blackness, he spoke.

"She's gone."

CHAPTER EIGHT

Julie woke early on Monday morning, showered and dressed, then left for the chemist's to collect the prescription the doctor had given her for Brian.

There was a young man behind the counter. He was about two years older than Julie, and he appeared to be in a foul temper. He took the note from Julie, read it, then frowned at her. "I'm sorry, I can't give you this," he said. "These are very strong pain-killers – I can't give pain-killers to a minor."

Julie was in no mood for him. Normally, she'd have just left the shop, embarrassed, but this time, after all she'd been through, she was ready for a fight. "Why not? There's no law against it."

"Look here, young lady, you can't just come marching in here looking for pain-killers. Get your mother or someone to come down for them."

Julie glared at him. "Is there another chemist's in town?"

He shook his head. "Even if there was, they'd say the same thing."

She gritted her teeth. "*Would* they?"

The chemist nodded. Julie reached over the counter, snatched the prescription from him, and headed towards the door.

"Come back here!" he called after her. "I was only joking!"

"Get lost!" Julie shouted. Slamming the door behind her, she stood in the street and tears welled up in her eyes. There was a phone box across the street. Julie thought about phoning the doctor. She had his card in her pocket.

The door to the chemist's opened, and the young man came out. "I'm sorry," he said. "I didn't mean anything by it. I'm not even a chemist. I'm just looking after the counter while my mother has her lunch."

Julie looked up at him. He genuinely did look sorry. He smiled at her, and she couldn't help smiling back. "It's okay," she said. She sniffed a little. "Then you'll give me the tablets?"

He smiled again. Julie decided it was a nice smile. "Of course I will. Come back inside."

He held the door open for her as she walked in. "Have a seat," he said, pointing to a stool in front of the prescriptions counter. "I'll get Mam to sort this out." He disappeared into a back room, and a few minutes later an older woman followed him out.

While his mother was rummaging through the jars and bottles, the young man stood next to Julie, and spoke quietly. "I'm really sorry about that, I must have woken up in a weird mood this morning."

"It's okay," Julie said. "I haven't been in the best of form lately myself."

"I haven't seen you around here before."

"I'm staying with my grandad, Tom Kavanagh."

"Up in that big old house? Isn't it lonely?"

She shook her head. "No, Grandad's there, and Brian." She thought about mentioning the ghost, but decided against it.

"So who's Brian?" he asked. "Your boyfriend?"

Julie laughed. "He's my cousin."

"So your boyfriend's not with you, then?"

Julie shrugged. She thought of Craig Kipling, but he wasn't even nearly her boyfriend, however much she wanted him to be. "I'm between boyfriends at the moment."

"I see," the young man said. Julie thought she saw him give a slight smile.

"I'm giving him grinds. He didn't do too well in the Junior Cert."

"I didn't know the results were out yet."

"They're not, but he said that he could only understand about one question in ten. He's not stupid, he just never bothered to study."

"I know the feeling. I'm Phil, by the way," he said, offering his hand.

Julie introduced herself and shook his hand.

Phil's mother returned to the counter with a small jar of pills, stuck a label on it and wrote a few instructions on the label. "There you go, love. Philip? Will you look after the register?"

After Phil's mother went back to the other room, Julie took her purse out of her pocket. "How much is it?"

Phil told her the price and said, "I'd give them to you free if I could, but my mother would go mad."

Julie smiled at him and handed over the money.

64

"Thanks, anyway." She noticed that he had deep brown eyes. She'd always liked brown eyes.

"So," he said. "Are you in a rush to get back?"

"No, no hurry."

"Would you like a cup of tea?" He smiled again, and Julie felt her heart melt.

She sighed. "I'd *love* a cup of tea."

* * *

Julie hummed to herself as she walked back to the house. She decided she liked Phil a lot, even more than Craig Kipling. Now that she thought about it, Craig always seemed a bit snobbish. Not at all like Phil.

They'd chatted for nearly half-an-hour, until Phil's mother, who owned the shop, had come in. Julie thought that he was just about to ask her out; they'd been talking about their favourite films, and the subject had just turned to the film currently showing in the local cinema, but Phil's mother returned from lunch and cut the conversation short.

Julie decided that she'd have to find another excuse to visit the chemist's.

On the way home, Julie stopped at the post office to post her letter to Maireád. She though about putting a postscript to the letter, telling Maireád about Phil, but decided against it. After all, it might come to nothing, and then Maireád would be full of questions about him that Julie knew she'd have a hard time answering.

It was a beautiful morning, and Julie took her time going back to the house. There were some wild roses growing by the side of the road, and Julie braved the thorns and picked a handful. She decided that if the roses died before Phil asked her out, then it wasn't meant to be and she'd forget about him.

She walked through the gate, and meandered slowly up the long, winding drive. Brian was sitting at the porch, reading and sipping occasionally from a can of *Sunkist*. He waved when he saw her.

"What kept you?" Brian asked.

Julie didn't answer. She just looked at him.

"What's the matter? Did something happen?"

Still she didn't move. She kept staring. Embarrassed, Brian rubbed his hand over his face, just in case one of his spots had started to bleed. Then he looked down in case his fly was open.

Julie continued staring at him. Her mouth had dropped open, and the blood drained out of her face, leaving her pale and gaunt. Then Brian realised. She wasn't looking *at* him. She was looking at something *behind* him.

He turned. Just inside the door a vague, unearthly shape was quickly fading away.

* * *

Brian grabbed Julie by the shoulders and shook her. "It's gone, it's gone."

Slowly, Julie returned to normal. She began to shake, and stammer. "It . . . it . . . Brian, I saw it. I saw it!"

"It's okay, Julie, it's gone now." He looked back at the doorway. There was nothing to indicate that the ghost had ever been there. He led Julie by the arm into the house, shivering when he passed where the ghost had been.

"Where's Grandad?" Julie asked. Her voice was shaking.

"He's in the kitchen. Come on." He opened the door to the living-room and brought her inside.

Julie sat down on the sofa, and Brian sat next to her. "It was like you said. Like my mother, only older, then younger. All ages. And it seemed to be in so much pain! Oh, God! Brian, what are we going to do?"

"Calm down. Look, Grandad can't find out about this, and if he sees you shaking he'll know we've seen it."

Julie took a deep breath. "You don't really think he killed her, do you?"

Brian laughed. "Of course not! But he's an old man; if he saw the ghost, well, he might have a heart attack, or something."

Julie found that even more terrifying than the sight of the ghost. "Is that why it's here?" she asked. "Grandad said that it always appears when someone is born or someone dies. Does it think that he's going to die?"

"I don't know. I hope not."

She began to cry.

Brian put his arm around her. "Julie, don't. Think of something different. Think of something nice."

Something nice. She sniffed and wiped her eyes, then noticed that she still had the wild roses in her other hand. She thought about Phil, and smiled.

Brian looked at her. "That was quick! What are you thinking about?"

"Oh, nothing." Julie said, still smiling. She held up the flowers. "Can you get me a vase to put these in?"

67

* * *

It had shown itself to the girl, and she had seemed to understand. But the girl's fear for her grandfather's life was preventing her from truly understanding.

It had to show them the pain it felt. It had to show them how they could help.

Somehow, it knew that it didn't have much time. Soon it would lose its contact with the mortal world, and be stranded forever, doomed to drift in the shadows for eternity.

The boy and girl were its last hope.

CHAPTER NINE

"What's the significance of Banquo's ghost sitting in Macbeth's place at the dinner table?" Julie asked.

"That's easy – Macbeth looks around, and sees that every place is full. He asked why there's no room for him, and they say that there is. They can't see the ghost."

Julie tutted. "If that's how you answered your questions in the Junior Cert I'm not surprised you're going to fail."

"Who said I'm going to fail? The results haven't come out yet."

"You said you couldn't understand most of the questions."

"Oh, I could understand the questions all right, I just didn't know the answers."

"Well, you ought to know this one."

Brian was exasperated. "I just answered it!"

"No, you didn't. You told me what happened. But what's the *significance* of the event?"

He shrugged. "It shows that he's hallucinating?" he offered.

"Nope."

Brian picked up two pencils, stuck them in his ears, and shook his head from side to side so that the pencils waggled. He pulled them out when he saw that Julie wasn't amused. "I give up."

"You can't give up. I want an answer. Now, think! What do the witches say to Banquo?"

"Em . . . 'Thou shalt get kings, though thou be none.'"

"Right. And what does that mean?"

"It means that Banquo won't become a king, but his descendants will."

Julie looked at him expectantly. "So . . ."

Brian's expression was blank. "So?"

"Come on, you work it out. Banquo's ghost is sitting in Macbeth's place, right?"

"Ah! So this indicates that Banquo's line will replace Macbeth!"

"Brilliant, Sherlock. How do you do it?" Julie voice was dripping with sarcasm.

Brian laughed. "Sedimentary, my dear Watson."

"You mean 'Elementary'."

Brian sighed and shook his head. "I know. That was a joke."

"Oh!" said Julie. "Ha ha ha. There, was that okay?"

"This is easy," Brian said. He ignored Julie's sneer. "What's the next question?"

"What's so important about Lady Macbeth's sleep-walking scene?"

Brian thought about this for a few seconds. "She's dreaming that she can't wash the blood off her hands. There's a doctor and a servant-woman watching her.

Macbetty says things like 'Who would have thought the old man had so much blood in him?' and 'Here's the smell of blood still: all the perfumes of Arabia will not sweeten this little hand.' After she goes back to bed, the doctor says 'Unnatural deeds do breed unnatural troubles', so he knows that she's been up to something. He then says 'More needs she the divine than the physician.'"

"Very good," Julie said. "You're certainly getting better at remembering your lines. But what's the point of the scene?"

"I was getting to that. It shows that Lady Macbeth isn't without a conscience. She's racked with guilt about killing Duncan, just like Macbeth is. Also, the doctor figures out what has happened. He says 'My mind she has mated, and amazed my sight: I think, but dare not speak.'"

Julie grinned and nodded. "Not bad. Now, write an account of Macbeth's second meeting with the witches, in not less than five hundred words."

Brian sighed. "Do I have to?"

"Look, Brian, in about two years you'll be doing this in the Leaving Cert. If you know it all now you're going to be two years ahead of everyone else. But if you don't bother with it now, you'll just keep putting it off, until one day you'll realise that the exam is the next day and you haven't done a scrap of work. Now, do you want to pass?"

Brian groaned, and picked up a pencil.

* * *

Father McCanney nodded politely as he listened to Tom's story. He didn't believe a word of it, but decided it was best to humour the old man. It was late on Monday afternoon, and they were sitting in the priest's chambers.

"Ever since the children came to stay it's been getting worse. I'm afraid that something might happen to them."

"Mr Kavanagh, has the . . . ghost . . . ever harmed anyone before?"

Tom shook his head.

"And you haven't noticed anything yourself?"

"Not lately, no."

"Have you considered the fact that they *are* only teenagers? Perhaps they're just making it up."

"I don't think so, Father. They're more scared by this than I am."

"So, what do you want me to do?"

Tom looked at him. "I want you to perform an exorcism."

The priest sat thoughtfully for a moment. "You do realise that an exorcism is one of the most difficult and dangerous of the holy rites to perform?"

"I know. I also know you need authorisation from the archbishop." Tom couldn't help smiling. "And getting permission from him might be even more difficult than performing the exorcism itself."

"I'll tell you what I can do, Mr Kavanagh. I'll go back with you, and see the house for myself. I'll bless every room. If there is something there, that might be enough."

"Thank you, Father. I'd appreciate that."

* * *

Julie and Brian were studying their grandfather's journal, hoping to find some clue that might help them free the ghost, when they heard him come in. Julie slammed the book closed and they both made a dive for the armchairs, trying to look as though they had been sitting there all evening.

The door opened and Grandad Tom walked in, closely followed by a tall young man wearing a priest's black uniform and white collar. "Julie, Brian," Grandad Tom said. "This is Father McCanney. He's going to help us get rid of the ghost."

Julie frowned. "I thought you said that you didn't want to get rid of it until you knew why it was here."

"I was wrong. There's been too much happening over the past few days." He walked over to his desk and sat down.

"Are you going to do an exorcism, Father?" Brian asked.

Father McCanney smiled. "I don't think so, Brian. What I really want to do is ask you both a few questions, then we'll go and bless the rooms."

Brian looked at Julie, who shrugged. "What do you need to know?" Brian asked.

The priest sat down on the sofa. "Have either of you ever encountered anything like this before?"

They both said that they hadn't.

Over the course of the next hour, Father McCanney asked Julie and Brian dozens of questions relating to the ghost. They'd avoided mentioning that both of them had actually seen it, and that they thought they knew what it was. The priest then took a bottle of holy water from his pocket, sprinkled some around the room, and read a few passages from his Bible. He made the sign of the cross, and asked them all to follow him through the house.

One by one, he blessed every room in the house, including the hall and both landings. When they reached Julie's room, the last to be blessed, Julie glanced nervously at the mirror. There were no marks in the dust.

Eventually, the priest gave them a short sermon on the supernatural, which he blended rather awkwardly into a lesson on morality. It was clear to Julie and Brian that Father McCanney didn't believe their story.

* * *

Grandad Tom walked the priest to the gate. "I don't think there's anything there, Mr Kavanagh."

"Why do you say that? Just because the holy water didn't boil away and the doors didn't slam in your face?"

Father McCanney laughed. "They're young, active teenagers, cooped up in a big old house that has a reputation for being haunted. Who can blame them if their imaginations run riot? I'm not saying they're lying, but I think they experience those things because they subconsciously *want* the house to be haunted."

"Father, they aren't the only ones who have heard and seen strange things in the house."

"Mr Kavanagh, I noticed that they are studying *Macbeth*. That play is full of the supernatural. And you said yourself that you'd been telling them about the alleged supernatural events that have happened over the years."

"I see," Tom said. "Well, thanks for your time. I'm sorry to bother you with all this."

The priest smiled and waved as he walked through the gate. "No trouble at all, Mr Kavanagh. Goodbye."

"Slán," Tom said. He turned back to the house. Maybe they *were* imagining it, he said to himself. Maybe we've *all* been imagining it.

* * *

Brian and Julie went back down to the living-room.

"He didn't believe us," Brian said.

"I don't blame him. I wouldn't have believed us either," Julie said. "We should have told him that we've actually seen the ghost."

"Why? He still wouldn't have believed us, and it would only have made things difficult for Grandad."

"We should have told him. It's the same as lying."

"Don't worry. I'm sure you can't go to hell for lying to a priest. At least, not when there's a good reason for it."

Julie shrugged. "So, now what do we do?"

"We'll have to wait to see if the ghost makes another appearance. It's trying to communicate with us. It might be able to tell us what we can do to help it."

Grandad Tom pushed open the front door and walked in. "Well," he said. "I hope that sorts everything out."

Julie scowled at him. "Grandad, after all your work! Don't you want to know what the ghost is?"

"Julie, I'm old. I've been trying to understand about this

75

ghost for most of my life, and I'm no nearer to the solution. It's got to end sometime." He opened the door. "I'm off to bed. We can talk about this in the morning, all right?"

Julie nodded. They said goodnight, and Grandad Tom closed the door behind him.

Brian waited until he heard the old man reach the top of the stairs before he spoke. "We have *got* to find out what the ghost needs."

"You're right," Julie said. "Maybe there's a way we can contact her." She looked around the room. "We could make a Ouija board."

Brian put up his hands. "No way! I've seen what those things can do!"

"This isn't one of your cheap video nasties, Brian. Besides, we know that the ghost doesn't mean any harm."

"That's not true. We don't know that at all."

"Well, *has* it harmed us?"

"I fell out of the tree," Brian said.

"That was your own stupid fault."

"I don't care. I'm not messing around with a wee-jee board, or what ever you call it."

"Ouija. The name comes from the French and German for 'Yes'; 'Oui' and 'Ja'. They're not dangerous if you know how to use them."

"But we don't know how to use one, do we?"

Julie had to admit that Brian was right. They talked about other ways to contact the ghost, but none of them seemed right. Eventually, Julie had an idea.

"I'm going to have a look at the mirror, see if there's any message on it."

"I'll come with you," Brian said.

They crept up the stairs as quietly as they could, and opened the door to Julie's room. Julie switched on the light, and looked at the mirror. There were no marks in the dust.

"Any other ideas?" Brian asked.

Julie shook her head. "Maybe when the priest blessed the rooms he got rid of the ghost."

"But is that a good thing, or a bad thing?"

"I wish I knew."

* * *

Father Peter McCanney sat up in bed, reading *Harpo Speaks!*, the autobiography of Harpo Marx. He chuckled to himself as he read some of the anecdotes: even though he considered himself an expert on the Marx Brothers, Father McCanney still loved to reread his favourite parts.

After a while, he put the book down and thought about Tom Kavanagh. The old man really did believe that there was a ghost in the house. Father McCanney shivered. Being a man of the cloth, he dealt with the supernatural on a daily basis, but he didn't believe in ghosts. When a body dies the soul leaves this universe and moves on, to Heaven or to Hell, whichever is appropriate. Or to purgatory, to do penance and await the Lord's forgiveness.

So where do ghosts come in to it? he asked himself. Some say they are the souls of people who have died, and can't move on to Heaven or Hell without getting rid of some unfinished business. He wondered where the ghost in Tom Kavanagh's house was waiting to go: Heaven or Hell? But there can't be many people who die *without* leaving unfinished business. No one ever says "I'm going to die in the morning, I'd better cancel the milk."

Father McCanney laughed at the idea. He picked up his notebook and pencil from their permanent place beside the bed to write down a brief description of the image. He decided it might be a good topic for a sermon. That was his approach to all his sermons – throw a few jokes in, make everyone realise that religion doesn't have to be as sour-looking as everyone seems to think.

He began to write, but his hand was shaking, and it wouldn't move the way he wanted it to. He stared in horror as his hand started to move across the paper of its own accord.

In big, awkward strokes, Father McCanney's hand formed the letter 'H'. His hand stopped moving, and he stared at the page. He couldn't believe what he'd just seen. Then his hand started to move again. This time it made the letter 'E'. He tried to let go of the pencil or the notebook, but he had no control over his hands.

The pencil moved again, writing a third capital letter, then a fourth. As it made the first vertical stroke down the page, Father McCanney leaned forward and gripped the pencil with his teeth. He pulled his head back, and the pencil slid away from the page, finishing the horizontal stroke on the fourth letter.

Father McCanney's hands were shaking. His fingers were cramped from holding the pencil so tight. He tried to move them, and this time his fingers flexed and his wrists bent; he had regained control over them.

Still shaking, Father McCanney looked down at his notebook, at the word written on the page. There was no denying it – the word was clear, and to the point. He knew where the ghost in Tom Kavanagh's house was waiting to go. He read the word aloud.

"HELL."

CHAPTER TEN

The ghost stood at the head of Julie's bed, watching her sleep. It tried to enter her mind, to read her dreams, but Julie's dreams were drifting, and vague.

It allowed itself to fade. The ghost knew it had achieved some success with the young priest, but it had lost so much of its power that it knew it couldn't attempt anything like that again for a long time.

It had always been tied to the house, the place that had been so important to it while it was alive. Leaving the house was tremendously difficult, and it had only managed it by lodging in the priest's mind. When the priest had broken its hold over him, the ghost had been pulled back to the house. This was its home.

It faded, and emerged in another time. It was daylight, and two young girls were sitting in their bedroom on the first floor. One was reading, the other playing with her dolls. They looked to be not more than ten years old. The ghost was struck at how alike the girls were, and also how like Julie they were.

Her mother and her aunt, the ghost said to itself. But which is which? It could not remember being in this time before.

It watched the girls at play. They didn't notice that there was another presence in the room. It found itself compelled to reach out and touch the girl playing with the dolls. This is Julie's mother, somehow I know that.

It left the girls, and drifted further back. It was night again, and snowing outside. The cousins' grandfather was sitting in the living-room, reading his journal. He was much younger, probably not more than forty. He still had most of his hair and was a good deal thinner. He continued reading as the ghost watched. He couldn't sense that he wasn't alone.

Again, the ghost drifted back in time. The grandfather was no more than a boy now. He was at the table in the kitchen, sitting with an older man and woman. His parents. The ghost examined the woman carefully. She, too, strongly resembled Julie. Is this who I was? The ghost wondered. Julie and Brian seem to think I was their great-grandmother. I have no memory of being her, but then I have no memory of being anybody. I feel that I have been in this house for an eternity.

It knew that change was coming. Its thoughts were more defined, its power was growing stronger, the pain of its half-existence was lessening. It had waited a long time, and it knew – or rather, it hoped; it prayed – that Julie would be able to help.

What will happen to me if this is ended? Is it true that there's a God, a Heaven to which I will go? Or is this all that there is? Maybe the mind and soul normally die with the body, fading like a clockwork toy winding down, but somehow my mind stayed active . . . I have been freed from the physical world and all its trappings. Even time cannot hold me. But this is still a prison.

It watched the boy chatting with his mother, while his father silently read the newspaper. *His father will be dead in ten years*, the ghost said to itself. *His mother seven years after that. Perhaps . . . perhaps I can visit the time of his father's death. Will his soul rise from the body, as people believe it does? Will I be able to see it?*

Will he be able to see me?

The ghost allowed its concentration to loosen, and again it slipped through time, pulled by the forces of strong emotions.

It was daylight, early morning. The house was packed with people, all laughing and eating and drinking, singing and dancing. *A wake?* It wondered. *No, not a wake . . . a party. A christening party.* There was a large cot tucked away in a quiet corner, with a baby girl asleep inside. Julie. The ghost peered closely, and the baby opened its eyes and looked straight at it.

The ghost would never have thought it could be startled by anything. Somehow, the baby seemed to know what it was looking at, and it started to cry. Julie's mother rushed into the room, and picked the baby girl up, rocking her gently in her arms. The ghost faded again, the memory of the baby's cry lingering and echoing. The ghost knew that the baby was crying not from fear, but from pity.

It was a few weeks before. The house was almost empty, only the housekeeper, Mrs Prentiss, was there. The ghost made its way to the front bedroom on the first floor. Mrs Prentiss was vacuuming the carpet, moving furniture out of the way and trying not to become entangled in the power cord.

The ghost watched her for a while. The company of

Mrs Prentiss was comforting. She was a rational and understanding woman, though the ghost wasn't sure how it knew this. It began to solidify its presence. Mrs Prentiss stopped, and looked around. Seeing nothing, she shivered and returned to work. She can sense me, the ghost said to itself. It continued watching her, waiting to see if the woman would turn around again.

Mrs Prentiss finished the vacuuming and pulled a yellow duster out of her apron pocket. She polished the bedsteads, the mantelpiece, the shelves. She is a good woman, the ghost thought. She works hard and puts up with a lot of trouble from Tom Kavanagh.

The housekeeper sprayed some foam cleaner on the room's large mirror, and began to polish it. The ghost watched, concentrating on the woman, not realising that it was becoming visible.

Mrs Prentiss dropped her duster and stared into the mirror. Realising that it had been seen, the ghost quickly faded. It felt the tug of emotions, drawing it once more to the real world. Ciarán Kavanagh, Tom's father, was lying in bed, alone. His breathing was shallow, and his eyes were misting. The ghost watched him. He's dying. He's dying and there's no one here for him. No one but me.

Ciarán Kavanagh looked around weakly and saw the ghost. His body relaxed, and he spoke.

"You. I have met you before. Do I know you?"

The ghost found that it could answer him. "I don't know. You can see me?"

He shook his head weakly. "I can see a glow, very faint. But I can sense you, like before."

"Who am I?"

"You don't know who you are?" Ciarán asked in surprise.

"I don't even know what I am."

"You're the ghost. You have been in this house for as long as I can remember. I saw you when I was a boy. You said that you would see me again, at the end of my life. Am I dying?"

"Yes. I'm sorry."

"Don't be. I've been happy. You were right. But . . . you were different then. You seemed to know everything." He shook his head slowly. "I thought that it was a dream."

"I do not remember. Perhaps it was a dream. Perhaps all of this is a dream."

"No. I'm dying, I know that." Ciarán Kavanagh lay back on the pillow. His eyes began to close. "All my life I have tried to do good. You showed me that death is real and it is something that touches every living thing. What happens after death?"

"No one knows."

"You must know. Tell me."

"I'm sorry. I have been trapped on this earth for so long."

"When did you die?"

"I don't know."

Ciarán's eyes opened again. "I'm not old. It's not right for me to die. Why is it that you have taken so long to come back to me? When it is too late for anyone to believe me?"

"Perhaps when we're dying our minds begin to open, to see all of existence, not just the human world."

"Is there a Heaven? Is there a God?"

The ghost looked sadly at his frail body. "I hope so."

Ciarán turned his eyes to the ghost once more. "Help me."

The ghost searched what little memory of human life it had. Then it placed its intangible hand on the dying man's forehead. "No one can be said to have lived a truly holy life. Do you repent before God?"

"I do." His voice was much weaker, barely a whisper. He closed his eyes.

"I absolve you of all your sins." The ghost looked at Ciarán Kavanagh's frail, empty body. "Rest in peace."

* * *

It remained in Ciarán Kavanagh's bedroom for five hours, waiting for someone to come home and find the body. Eventually, Tom arrived. He was only fourteen years old. The ghost left the grief-stricken boy, and faded through time once more.

The house was still being built. The foundations had been set, and most of the materials were piled up in what was to become the front garden. A group of young boys had made a see-saw from a thick plank and a stack of house bricks. They climbed around the foundations and dared each other to jump from the top of one half-built wall onto a pile of waiting sand.

The ghost watched them passively. After a few minutes, one of the boys shouted a warning, and they all disappeared across the field. A teenage boy arrived. He chased them part of the way, then came back. He looked around the site, and seeing that no damage had been done, began to walk away.

The ghost looked at the boy's face. It was Ciarán Kavanagh. *This is the time,* it said to itself, *this is the time he spoke of.*

It moved in front of the boy, and tried to concentrate on becoming visible, though it knew that all he could see was a shimmering light. The boy stopped, startled. He began to back away.

"Stop!" The ghost said, surprised to find that its voice was real. "I must talk with you, Ciarán."

Ciarán swallowed. "What are you? What do you want with me?"

The ghost could not think of what to say. It could not tell him that he would die alone, in his bed, at the age of fifty. But maybe that is exactly what it should do. "Every living thing, Ciarán, has something in common. That is death. I have seen your death, Ciarán Kavanagh. Your life must not be wasted. This house; it can be your kingdom."

Ciarán shook his head. "I don't understand. This is not my house, I'm only a builder. My family could never afford something like this."

"This house will be your legacy, to your children, your grandchildren, your great-grandchildren. You must work hard, Ciarán, work well. This house *will* be yours, I have seen it."

"When will I die?"

"I cannot tell you that. But you will be happy. And loved, very much loved."

Ciarán looked around. "Is this real? Is this really happening?"

The ghost smiled, it knew that it had succeeded. "That is for you to decide."

It began to fade.

"Wait! Don't go! Will I see you again?"

"I will be here. And you will see me again, at the end of your life."

The ghost watched as the scene faded to black.

* * *

I have shaped his life, the ghost said to itself. Ciarán Kavanagh was the start of this clan, and I have directed him. I have helped form the start of this family. That was why I was brought to his death bed. I had work to do.

The ghost found itself back in Julie's bedroom. The girl was still asleep, unaware of the ghost standing over her. And is that why I am here? Is there work for me in this time? Perhaps it is not for them to help me, but for me to help them.

I have been guided to this girl, because she needs me. But that leaves a question to which I have no answer.

I have guided Ciarán Kavanagh, and I am here to guide his descendant Julie Logan. But . . .

But who is guiding me?

CHAPTER ELEVEN

Brian and Julie sat in the living-room, going over the geography that Brian should have learned for the Junior Cert.

"Can you name all of the states in the USA?" Julie asked.

"No, I can't, and that's the right answer."

"Seriously, Brian. This is the stuff you need to know."

"Oh yeah? How come I've never seen an exam paper that asks that particular question? Or asks you to name all the counties in Ireland?"

Julie sighed. "Brian, this isn't about just passing exams. You don't go to school just so you can learn enough to pass the tests and get a good job. The whole idea is that you learn things that will be useful in the real world."

Brian smirked. "Really? Give me one good example of how knowing the names of all the states is useful."

"Well, first of all . . ." Julie paused. She couldn't think of an example.

Brian laughed. "See? I told you."

"Right. Okay. In school we learn geography so we can pass geography exams. Everything else has a real purpose. I want you to know the names of all the states by tomorrow."

Brian hunched up one shoulder and let his arm swing loosely by his side. He tilted his head and crossed his eyes. "Yes, master."

Julie couldn't help laughing at him. "I wish you'd take this more seriously."

"What's the next question? I might know the answer."

"I'm sure." She checked her notes. "What is the capital of Finland, and what body of water is it closest to?"

Brian thought about the question for a few seconds. "The capital of Finland is . . . 'F'"

Julie gritted her teeth. "Brian!"

"Okay, okay! The capital of Finland is Helsinki, and the closest body of water is . . . The Baltic Sea?"

Julie tutted and shook her head. "Learn that by tomorrow, too."

Brian shrugged. "I was right about the capital."

"All right then, what's the capital of Australia?"

"Melbourne."

Julie shook her head. "No."

"Sydney?"

"Nope."

"Em . . . Alice Springs?"

"Not even close."

"All right, I give up."

"It's Canberra."

Brian raised an eyebrow. "You're having me on. Canberra! What sort of a name is that?"

"It's the name of the capital of Australia, that's what. Look it up. What's the name of the canal that flows through Egypt, linking the Mediterranean with the Red Sea? And while we're at it, what's the capital of Egypt?"

"The Suez Canal, and the capital is Cairo."

Julie nodded. "Not bad. Okay, where does the –"

They were interrupted by the arrival of Mrs Prentiss, trailing a vacuum cleaner behind her. "I'm just going to do in here, don't mind me."

Julie stood up. "No, it's all right, Mrs Prentiss. We're due a break, anyway. We've been at this for nearly four hours." She glanced at the wild roses that were in a vase on the mantelpiece. "I think I'll go for a little walk to the shops," she said, trying to make it sound as casual as possible.

"Good idea," Brian said. "I'll go with you."

"No, you'd better keep studying."

"Ah, I can study later. I want to see if I can find a shop that sells my computer magazine."

"What's it called?" Julie said. "I'll have a look for it."

"Thanks, but I'll go myself."

Julie shrugged, pretending that she didn't care if Brian came along. "Suit yourself."

Mrs Prentiss looked up. "If you want to wait an hour or so, I'm about to make lunch."

"Great," said Julie. "Thanks. I'll give you a hand." This will give me some time to think of a way to make Brian stay here, she said to herself.

* * *

89

Brian disappeared into his bedroom to study while Julie and Mrs Prentiss were preparing lunch. "He's just trying to get out of helping us," Julie said. She finished buttering the bread, and began to slice a tomato.

"He's just like his grandfather," Mrs Prentiss said. "And speaking of the lord and master, where is he today?"

"Fishing again," Julie said.

Mrs Prentiss grinned slyly. "Ah, fishing! Have you ever noticed how he never catches anything?"

"Grandad says that he doesn't like hurting the fish, he just goes for the peace and quiet. Sometime he meets his friends there."

The housekeeper laughed. "They're a great lot for 'fishing' in this town, I can tell you."

Julie finished making the sandwiches, and carried them over to the kitchen table. "You've been working for Grandad a long time, haven't you?"

"Nearly twenty years, now. After your grandmother died, he needed someone to look after him."

"What was she like? My grandmother, I mean."

Mrs Prentiss poured out two cups of tea. "I didn't know her that well, only to see. But everyone thought she was a lovely woman. Very beautiful. The twins got their looks from their father's side of the family, though that's not to say they weren't good-looking too."

They sat down to eat. "Shouldn't we tell Brian it's ready?" Julie said.

"What! And have him eat the lot? Let him wait. If he was that hungry, he'd have helped us."

Julie smiled. "You know, I didn't like him at all until we came here, but he's not that bad."

"Most people aren't too bad, if you get to know them in the right circumstances. Now then, are you going to tell me why you don't want Brian to go to the shops with you?"

Julie felt herself blushing. "Was it that obvious?"

"It was to me, but then I remember your mother doing the same to Carol, when she was a little older than you are now. Trying to keep this fella a secret, eh?"

"Well, I was. I just met him yesterday, and I think he really likes me. His name's Phil, he works in the chemist's."

"Ah, that would be Marie Hudson's lad. Quiet fellow, tall, brown hair?"

Julie nodded. "That's him."

"I was talking to Marie yesterday. Nosy old cow, she is. She said Philip was mooning around the house, even ironed his own shirts. She said there was a young one in the shop yesterday morning. She said she thought it must have been you."

"That was me. I was getting the prescription for Brian."

Mrs Prentiss sipped at her tea. "You know, I don't think Brian should be walking around town today. He told me that the doctor said he was to take it easy."

Julie grinned. "I hadn't thought of that!"

"There you are, now. I'm not just a silly old woman. I do have my uses."

"You certainly do," Julie said. "Does everyone know that we're staying here?"

"There's not much that gets past some of the folk round here," Mrs Prentiss said. "Gossip spreads like wildfire. My husband, Lord have mercy on him, used to say that things in this town were no sooner done than said."

Julie laughed. "Is it really that bad?"

"Well, I'm not one for gossip myself, but I've heard that Marie Hudson and Mrs O'Toole from the butcher's were awarded a civic medal for spying on the enemy during the war. Don't laugh, dear, or tomorrow they'll be talking about how Tom Kavanagh's granddaughter can't keep a straight face. I'm half-convinced there's a hidden camera in every house."

"Tell me about Phil, then."

Mrs Prentiss shrugged. "I don't know much about him myself. He's supposed to be very bright, but he's a bit on the shy side. His mother wants him to take over the chemist's when she retires, but he wants to be an astronaut."

"An *astronaut*?"

Mrs Prentiss nodded. "Yes. Or was it an acrobat? Something beginning with 'A', anyway. Now, hurry up and finish your lunch, dear. Then run along and see your young man. I'll deal with Brian."

"You're very kind, Mrs Prentiss."

"Not at all." She paused. "I want to talk to you later on, though. I'll be back around three."

"Is it anything important?"

"No, no. It can wait."

Julie finished her lunch, then started to clear away the plates.

"Leave that, Julie. I'll do it later."

"Are you sure?"

"Of course, now hurry. You don't want someone else to get there before you, do you?"

Mrs Prentiss watched Julie walk down the drive. She returned to the kitchen and poured herself another cup of tea. She drank it slowly, going over in her mind the questions she wanted to ask Julie.

Why did Father McCanney visit the house last night? And had it anything to do with the fact that he had failed to turn up for Mass this morning?

CHAPTER TWELVE

"I need to speak to the archbishop," Father McCanney said.

The archbishop's assistant looked sourly at the young priest. "I'm afraid His Reverence is rather busy at the moment. He couldn't possibly see anyone without an appointment. Perhaps you could leave a message for him?"

Father McCanney ground his teeth in annoyance. "This is rather important. Is there no way . . .?"

"I'm sorry, no. He left word that he was not to be disturbed. Can you tell me why you wish to see him?"

The young priest looked at his right hand. It was still shaking, and had been since the previous night, but he hoped that this was merely due to shock. How can I tell anyone about this? he wondered. Who will believe me? Even the archbishop is probably too wrapped up in the real world to believe I've been possessed by a ghost.

The archbishop's assistant regarded him curiously. "Is everything all right, Father?"

Father McCanney took a deep breath. "Yes, yes, thank you. Everything's fine." He glanced around the room. "It's not important. I'll see His Reverence another time. Or I'll phone him. That's what I'll do. Thanks for your time." He moved towards the door. "I'm sorry to bother you."

"Not at all. Good day, Father McCanney. God bless."

Father McCanney nodded absently and left the room.

He stood in the corridor, wondering what to do next. He could talk to Father Mitchell, the parish priest, but he too was likely to be busy, helping to organise the upcoming summer festival.

The bus home was crowded with shoppers and schoolchildren. Not for the first time Father McCanney envied those priests who'd been assigned more affluent parishes, and who were able to afford cars. Then he smiled to himself. Envy is one of the seven deadly sins. Bless me, Father, he said to himself, for I have sinned. And what is your sin, my son? I have envied my friend Father Dennehy in Castlemorris who has a Nissan Micra, and I have wished I had a Saab Turbo so I could carve him up on the road. For your penance, say three thousand Hail Marys and drive more safely in future.

He sat at the back of the bus, downstairs, watching the passengers. He mentally placed bets as to which passenger would be getting off at which stop. He was right once, and in his mind a crowd cheered, then he got to shake Mike Murphy's hand and was awarded a Saab Turbo.

After what had seemed a lifetime's journey on the bus, Father McCanney made it home. He went up to his room and took the notebook out of his pocket. He opened it and looked at the first page. HELL. He ran his fingers over the page. The pencil marks were so deep that he'd be seeing the word indented into the pages for a long time.

There was a knock on the door. Father McCanney closed the notebook, then said "Come in!"

It was Father Mitchell. The elderly parish priest was an understanding man, though often a bit impatient. "Good afternoon, Peter," he said frostily. "I trust your business with the archbishop went well?"

Father McCanney shook his head. "I didn't get to see him, Robert. He was too busy."

Father Mitchell sat down on the bed. "Are you going to tell me what this is all about?"

"To be honest, I don't think you'd believe me."

"You never know. But remember, if there's anything wrong, it's your duty to tell me. Either here or in the confessional."

"I know. Thank you." He hesitated. "And thank you for standing in for me this morning. I'll do the evening service for you tonight."

"Fine. You *will* let me know what's going on, won't you?" Father Mitchell stood up to leave.

"In time, Robert. I'm not sure what's going on myself."

"Very well." He opened the door. "Five-thirty, don't forget."

"I won't. Thanks again."

Father Mitchell closed the door behind him, leaving Father McCanney looking at his notebook, then at his hand, and back to the notebook again. He remembered his earlier conversation with Father Mitchell.

"There *is* something out there for me, Father," he said to himself, "and, God help me, I think I've found it."

* * *

"Hey, Grandad! How's it going?" Brian said, standing in the doorway of the living-room.

"Not too bad, Brian," said his grandfather, removing his jacket and putting away his umbrella. He put his fishing gear away in the press under the stairs. "What's this? Not studying?" He pushed past Brian into the living-room.

"I was, until I heard you come in. Mrs Prentiss said she'll be back later, and Julie's gone to the shops, left me to study on my own."

Grandad Tom laughed. "You poor boy! Turning those heavy pages all by yourself. I'll tell you what, I'll allow you to have ten minutes off, on one condition."

Brian grinned. "Would this condition have anything to do with hot water and tea bags?"

"You're reading people's minds again, boy. Nasty habit. You are hereby banished to the kitchen until such time as the kettle has boiled and the tea has been made."

Brian went into the kitchen, leaving the door open so he could talk to his grandfather. "So, did you catch anything?"

"No, nothing," Grandad Tom called back.

"I'm beginning to think that there aren't any fish in that river," Brian said.

"Tell me, how's the studying going?"

"Not bad." Brian returned to the living-room. "It's a lot easier if you have a personal tutor."

"I'm sure it is. Have you decided what you're going to get for Julie?"

97

Brian was surprised at the question. "Get something for Julie? What do you mean?"

Grandad Tom tutted. "Brian, she's doing all this work for you, and you haven't thought of getting her anything in return. I'm sure you've got money with you. Buy her a box of chocolates, or flowers, or something."

Brian felt a sudden attack of guilt. "I'm glad you mentioned it. I wouldn't have thought of it myself. What do you think I should do?"

"I think . . . I think you should see if the kettle's boiled yet, and make your grandad a cup of tea, there's a good lad."

* * *

Julie had walked past the chemist's five times, and each time there had been customers in the shop. The last time, she'd gone into the phone box across the street, and pretended to make a call while she waited for the shop to clear.

She stood in the phone box, with the receiver cradled in her shoulder, quietly reciting a poem, in case anyone should look in and see that she wasn't talking. She looked across the street, and groaned. The chemist's had closed; the shutters were down, and the lights were off.

Someone knocked on the door of the phone box. Still trying to pretend to be making a call, Julie spoke loudly. "Well, I've got to go, someone wants to use the phone . . . no, I won't forget, bye . . . what? Yeah, I will, thanks . . . okay, bye." She hung up, and turned to the door. Phil was standing outside the box, looking in and grinning.

Julie opened the door. "Hi! Did you want to use the phone?"

"No, I just saw you there. I came over to say hello."
He smiled.

Julie smiled back, feeling rather awkward. "Hello."

"I've just closed up for lunch," Phil said. "Are you
hungry?"

She thought of the sandwiches she'd had for lunch,
less than an hour before. "I'm starving," she lied.

"Great! There's a little café just around the corner
and down the road a bit. Would you like to join me?"

"Well, I was supposed to be meeting the president for
lunch, but she cancelled at the last minute. Typical. So I
do find myself free for the next hour or so."

They walked side by side down the street. "So," Phil
said. "Who were you calling."

"Oh, nobody."

Phil laughed. "You were in the phone box for ten
minutes talking to nobody?"

Julie blushed. "I mean, nobody important."

"So it wasn't the president or the pope or Christian
Slater or anybody like that?"

She laughed. "No, just Mairéad, my best friend."

"I though you might be ringing your boyfriend, or
something."

Julie stopped and looked at him. "Didn't we go
through all this before?"

Phil grinned, and winked at her. "Just checking."
They continued walking.

"So, what about you?" Julie asked. "Have you got a
girlfriend?"

"No, sure who'd have me?"

Julie said nothing. They'd reached the café, and Phil

bought some sandwiches and two Cokes, then they sat down at a table by the window.

"I hope you like salad sandwiches," Phil said. "It's about the only thing in here that you can trust."

Julie looked at the pile of sandwiches in front of her. "Great, thanks," she said, with as much enthusiasm as she could muster. "Phil, do you believe in ghosts?"

"No. Do you believe in UFOs?"

"I'm serious. Really, do you believe in ghosts?"

"Well, I normally make it a personal policy not to disregard anything. There are too many unexplained things in this world. But *ghosts*. Rattling chains, strange noises, passing through walls . . . no, I don't believe in them. Why do you ask?" He picked up a sandwich and demolished it in three bites.

"Would you think I was mad if I said *I* believed in ghosts?"

Phil swallowed the rest of his sandwich. "No, but I'd think you were mad if you said 'Wibble, wibble, I'm a Christmas tree'." He paused. "So why do you ask?"

"Oh, I'm just curious. Brian and I were talking about ghosts this morning, and it's been on my mind."

"How is the teaching getting on?"

"Not too bad. He's fairly bright, but he'd rather annoy me or play games on his computer than actually do any work."

"Ah! What sort of a computer has he got?"

Julie shrugged. "He's just got a *Gameboy* with him, but he's got a bigger one at home. I can't remember the name. It begins with 'A', a foreign name."

"Amiga? Atari?" Phil offered.

"Yes, that's the one. Amiga. He wants me to get his magazine for him, if I can find it."

"Well, you won't have any luck here. There isn't a shop in town that sells computer magazines."

"So there's no point in looking?"

"Nope. Are you eating those?" Phil pointed to Julie's untouched sandwiches.

Julie looked at them guiltily. "I guess I wasn't as hungry as I thought. Go ahead."

"Thanks." Phil wolfed into the sandwiches.

Julie watched him as he ate. He's not bad-looking, she said to herself. Not bad-looking at all. And he's clever, and funny. She sighed. How would he be interested in me?

"On Thursday," Phil said, finishing off the last sandwich, "the summer festival is starting. There's a disco on in the school."

Julie swallowed. This is it! My God, he's going to ask me out!

"Everybody's going to be there," Phil said.

She waited. Her heart was beating loudly.

"So if you're interested in going along . . ."

Julie closed her eyes. I will remember this moment for the rest of my life, she thought.

" . . . I've got a couple of free tickets. They give some to every shop who helps sponsor the festival. Yourself and Brian could go."

Julie felt her heart sink. "Brian can't go," she said quickly. "The doctor said he was supposed to take it easy."

Phil shrugged. "Oh, well, you can have the tickets anyway, if you don't mind going on your own."

"On my own!" She couldn't believe what she was hearing.

"Well, you might find someone to bring before then, I suppose."

Julie thought she was going to cry. "But what about you?"

He laughed. "Oh, don't worry about me! I'm going to the cinema. I don't like discos much."

Julie grabbed Phil's wrist and looked at his watch. "Gosh, is that the time? Well, thanks for lunch. I'd better get back. Maybe I'll see you before I go back home." She stood up and picked up her bag. "Maybe."

Phil watched Julie as she walked up the street. Well, he said to himself, that could have gone better.

He finished his Coke, and left the café. He turned the corner at the top of the street to find Julie waiting outside the shop.

"Can I have those tickets?" Julie asked. "I've just remembered that there is someone I want to bring to the disco."

Phil didn't know what to say. He fished in his pocket, and took out his wallet. He handed Julie the tickets.

"Thanks," Julie said.

"So who are you going to bring?" Phil asked.

Julie looked at the tickets. "Eight o'clock, on Thursday. I'll be here at half seven. Be ready."

Phil paused. "You want *me* to go to the disco with you? Me?"

She scowled at him. "Yes, you. Or don't you want to go out with me?"

He was flustered. "Well, yes, I do, I'd be mad not to, but . . . I didn't think you'd want to go out with me."

Julie smiled. "You have a bad self-image. Well, do you want to go or not?"

"I'd love to. Thank you."

They stood looking at each other for a few awkward seconds. Julie shrugged. "I really do have to go."

"Okay. I'll see you on Thursday night, then. At half-seven." Phil hesitated, then leaned forward and kissed Julie on the cheek.

* * *

When Julie got back to the house and went into the living-room, Brian and Grandad Tom just looked at her and said hello. The three of them chatted casually for a while, but Julie couldn't believe that they didn't notice how nervous she was.

"So, did you get my magazine?" Brian asked.

"No, sorry. There isn't a shop in town that sells computer magazines." She reached into her pocket and handed him back his four pounds. "It's a lot of money for one magazine."

Brian shrugged. "They usually have a disk on the cover. I suppose that's where the money really goes."

Grandad Tom looked up from his book. "Speaking of computers, I was thinking about –" He was interrupted by the ringing of the phone.

"I'll get it!" Julie said, jumping up and running out to the hall.

She picked up the receiver. "Hello?"

"Julie? This is Carol, how are you?"

"Carol, hi! How's the weather?"

"It's great. I'm sitting by the pool at the moment, Billy's just brought me a drink." There was a sipping sound from the other end of the phone. "Susan's here, do you want to talk to her?"

"Sure!" There was a brief pause, then Julie's mother came on the line.

"Hi! How's it going?"

"Fine, couldn't be better," Julie said. "How's Dad?"

"Your father, believe it or not, went hang-gliding yesterday. Sacred me half to death."

Julie laughed. "Dad? Hang-gliding? I'd never have imagined it. How are you getting on with the Doyles?"

Her mother spoke softly, so no one would overhear. "They're driving me *mad*! Gemma and Keith keep jumping into the pool beside me. They're ruining my tan. Oh, I'm sorry, Julie. I wasn't thinking. It can't be much fun for you, stuck there with Brian."

"It's okay, Mam. He's not so bad."

"Listen, I'd better go. Can you get Brian? Carol wants to talk to him."

"Okay, see you when you get back."

Julie called Brian out to the phone and went back into the living-room.

"It's Mam," she told her grandfather. "They're having a great time."

Grandad Tom smiled at her. "Don't worry, love. Maybe it'll be your turn next year."

"Oh, I'm not worried. I'm enjoying myself here."

"Really? Even with the ghost and all that?"

Julie shrugged. "Maybe *because* of the ghost. I don't know . . . it's not every holiday that you come across a real ghost."

"That's true. Have you seen or heard anything lately?"

"No," Julie said. "Not for a few days. It's strange, now it hardly seems like anything really happened, but when I saw the ghost it was as real as the rest of us."

Grandad Tom looked at her. "You *saw* the ghost? When was this? Why didn't you tell me?"

Damn, Julie said to herself, now I've done it! She blushed. "I'm sorry, Grandad, we didn't want to worry you."

Julie could see that he was becoming more and more angry. "Worry me? It's been my life's work! No one has ever really seen the ghost before. What did it look like? Is it male or female? Young or old?"

She sighed. There was no point in denying anything now. "We'd better wait until Brian comes back in. He saw it first."

The old man shook his head. "Brian saw it too? I don't believe this. You should have told me." They sat in silence until Brian came in off the phone.

"Guess what?" Brian said. "Dad got me a whole load of software for my Amiga! He says it's dirt cheap over there. I gave him a list of games I wanted, and he's going to have a look for them tomorrow. He said that they . . ." Brian's voice trailed off as he noticed that both Julie and Grandad Tom were staring angrily at him. "What? What have I done now?"

"You never told me you'd seen the ghost," Grandad Tom said.

"Ah," Brian said. He gave Julie a scathing look. "Someone let it slip, then."

"Sit down, Brian. I want you to tell me about it."

Brian sat down on the sofa. "Grandad, you're not going to like it."

MICHAEL CARROLL

"I don't care. Tell me what you saw."

Brian looked at Julie, who nodded. "It was on Sunday, when I was climbing the tree to get my kite back. I saw it standing in the kitchen. It scared the hell out of me, that's what made me fall. Vague, shimmering, changing all the time. But one's thing's for sure; it was a woman."

His grandfather nodded, and began writing in his notebook. "A woman. Young or old?"

"I don't know. I mean, it was changing all the time, it was young, then old, then middle-aged, then young again. It didn't seem to have any particular age at any stage."

"Well, about how old and how young did it get?"

"About sixty or seventy at the oldest, about seven or eight at the youngest."

"So it changed from being a little girl to an old woman? Were these changes constant? I mean, was it growing old, then young, repeating the pattern, or was it random?"

"Random," Brian said. "It was like one image morphing into another."

Grandad Tom looked up at him, and raised his eyebrows quizzically. "Morphing? What's that?"

"Sorry. It's a computer term. It's when they have an image of something, and they get a computer to change it into something else. Like on those ads for computer games, or in videos. You see it all the time in science fiction movies."

"Well, not having a television set, I've never seen that sort of thing, but I think I know what you mean. I presume the term comes from the word 'metamorphic',

106

meaning a change of form. Julie, is that what you saw?"

Julie nodded. "The same thing. As if the ghost wasn't able to stay in one shape. I saw it yesterday morning, when I got back from the chemist's. It seemed like it was trying to come up with a shape we'd recognise."

Grandad Tom continued writing. "So, *did* you recognise it?"

Julie glanced at Brian. He looked back at her, and said "I think we should tell him."

"Tell me what?"

Julie took a deep breath, then sighed heavily. "Grandad, it looked like me, and my mother, and Carol, and when it was a child it was the image of Brian's sister."

Grandad Tom dropped his pen. His face had lost its colour. "Oh, my God. Are you sure?" His voice was very weak.

"I'm sure," Julie said. "When it was older, it looked like the photographs of your mother."

The old man swallowed heavily. Tears were coming to his eyes. "I never really thought it could be her. The ghost was around long before she died. My father said he saw the ghost when he was about sixteen." He sniffed to hold back the tears. "I was only twenty-one when she died. After that, I thought it might have been her ghost, but I remembered what my father said."

Julie walked over to her grandfather and put her arms around him. "Grandad, we can help her. We can find out why she's here and release her spirit."

He nodded, and wiped away his tears with his sleeve. He gave a short laugh. "Imagine an old man like me

107

crying. I have to write this up in the journal. Can you leave me alone for a few minutes?"

Brian and Julie left the room and went into the kitchen. "What will we do now?" Brian asked.

"We'll have to ask him how his mother died."

"I've been thinking about that. Look, if she died from something natural, like old age, there must be some other reason why her ghost has been left behind. We'll have to find out what it is."

"She's becoming stronger. No one has ever seen her before, right? At least, not like *we* have, anyway. And she's never tried to communicate before. Maybe she'll be able to let us know herself."

"I hope so," Brian said. "Otherwise she could be stuck here forever."

* * *

The ghost had listened to their conversation. I still cannot remember my past, it said to itself. But they must be right. The old man, their grandfather – was he my son?

Then Ciarán Kavanagh . . . he was my husband. But he didn't recognise me. Perhaps in his dying state he couldn't see me properly. No, the room was dark, and he said that all he could see was a glow.

But his son, Tom. I must show myself to him. He and the children can help me. They must help me, and soon. My time is running out.

In their world, time is constant. It travels in a straight line, and they have so little of it left, before . . .

Before what? The ghost didn't know what was to

happen. It only knew, somehow, that a great tragedy would befall them. I am here to help them, it said to itself. That is my purpose.

* * *

"Julie! Brian!" Grandad Tom shouted from the living-room. "Quickly!"

They rushed into the other room. Their grandfather was staring at his journal. His hand was shaking. "It happened all by itself," he said. "I was writing about what you said had happened, and something seemed to take control of my hand. Look." He held up the journal.

Written across the page, in large, awkward letters, were two words.

Julie shivered as she read them aloud.

"Help me."

CHAPTER THIRTEEN

"Tell me, Grandad, how did your mother die?" Julie asked.

"She had a heart attack. She was still young, only fifty-five. She always seemed healthy, never any sort of pain or anything, then one day she just died."

Brian glanced at Julie, then back at his grandfather. "Can you think of any reason why her ghost might have been left behind?"

Grandad Tom shook his head slowly. "No. She was happy, until my father died, at least. I was twenty-one, living in London, when I received a telegram saying that she'd had a heart attack, and I was to come home. By the time I got back here she was gone. I felt terrible, not just because she died, but because she died alone. When I came back, I decided to stay."

"Even though you were the only one here?" Julie asked.

He nodded, then smiled. "Well, if I'd stayed in England, I'd never have met your grandmother."

"We were talking about this earlier, Grandad," Julie said. "I think the ghost is getting stronger. I mean, she's never tried to communicate before. And Brian and I saw her, you said that's the first time."

"As far as I know, yes, apart from my father seeing her when he was younger." He looked at the page in his journal. "If she can help us to find out what she needs . . . no. I'm still not convinced that it's my mother. My father said he saw the ghost. Strange things have been happening since long before my mother died."

Brian shrugged. "Well, if ghosts aren't bound by the normal laws of the universe, who says they're bound by time?"

Julie turned to him. "What do you mean?"

"Everyone takes time for granted. One thing happens after another. But time is relative, Einstein proved that, right?" He noticed the blank looks from Julie and Grandad Tom. "Okay. Look, imagine you go to a planet with much higher gravity than ours, and you bring your watch with you. You stay there for a week, according to your watch, and come back. Less than a week will have passed for everyone else. That's assuming that the gravity isn't so strong that you'll be squashed to death. Get it?"

"No," Julie said.

"I'll give you a better example. You put a page into a photocopier, okay? The copier scans the page and prints a copy of the same size. The copier assumes that the page is a particular size, and it scans the page for exactly that length. If you put in a page that's twice as long, and move it while the copier is scanning, the copier will print out a squashed copy."

"I understand that, all right," Julie said. "But what's the connection with the ghost?"

"There's no connection with the ghost, this is about relativity. To the copier, the page is a standard length. It doesn't know that it's seeing twice as much. The length of the page is relative to the copier. Time works the same way, sort of. An hour is an hour to us, but time is flexible. If you were in a starship travelling at close to the speed of light, you might age at only a tenth of the rate of anyone else. Time is warped." He grinned. "Ta daa!"

Grandad Tom nodded. "So what you're saying, in your roundabout and mostly irrelevant way, is that time is one of the physical properties of the universe, so something not affected by those properties isn't necessarily confined to time the way we are."

Brian was exasperated. "That's what I said in the first place."

"So the ghost could go to any time it wanted?" Julie said.

"Probably," Grandad Tom said. "This is all conjecture, of course. But it makes sense, from that point of view."

"Then if the ghost is your mother, Grandad, it could easily visit any time it wanted to – back to the past, or even into the future. You said your father saw the ghost when he was only seventeen; it might have been his future wife." She sighed. "I think that's really romantic."

"I don't know about that, Julie," her grandfather said. "But I think Brian's got a point. Well done, lad. Your theory fits a lot better than any I've ever come up with myself."

Brian grinned. "Yes! Another difficult case solved by Detective Sherlock Doyle."

* * *

The ghost watched them. It was pleased with their progress, but it was concerned that they needed it to help them.

It still did not know why it was here. It couldn't even guess at how long it had been drifting into and out of the human world. Time was relative, and when you can go to any time you wish, it's hard to know how long you have been in existence.

The ghost decided to let go of the world once again, and allow itself to be pulled through time.

It was night. The house was quiet, dark, and empty. The ghost wondered why it had been called to this time. There was nothing here to see. For the first time that the ghost had known, the house was empty overnight. This is their future. Why is the house empty?

It stood in the front upstairs bedroom. There was the presence of another in the room, but the ghost couldn't see anything.

Then, slowly, a shape emerged from the shadows. The ghost recognised it as itself.

"You are my future," the ghost said. "You cannot be my past, as I do not remember a meeting like this before."

The other ghost seemed to nod. "I am your future. I remember this encounter, from your point of view."

"Will they succeed?"

It smiled. "Yes. They are very close, success is only days away. But there is still danger."

"Danger? To the children?"

"And to you. *Beware the young priest. His intentions are good, but he can cause much pain. You must guide him. Also, watch the boy Philip Hudson. He is a distraction to Julie. She is the one you need.*"

"But if there is danger, and you have warned me of it, does that not change things?"

The other ghost smiled. "No. You see, I was warned of it too."

"Why are you here? Why did you locate me? Was it just to give me riddles?"

"I too remember asking that. I am here to help you, but I can tell you only one more thing."

"What is that?"

The future ghost began to fade. "Go further. Much further. At least twenty years . . . you will see. You will see . . ."

It was gone. The ghost waited, alone. Then it also faded, and gathered its energies to project itself into the future.

Sunlight streamed through the partially-opened curtains in the bedroom. The ghost could hear children playing outside. It drifted through the house, and stopped when it saw a woman sitting in the living-room.

It is Julie's mother, or her aunt, the ghost said to itself. *But, no, it can't be, they would be much older by now. This woman must be Julie herself.*

Julie looked up. "Who's there?"

The ghost saw her shiver and return to her book. *She is so like her mother,* the ghost thought. *Remarkably like her mother. She has children of her own now, and she seems happy.*

Does this mean that all will turn out well?

Shortly, Julie put her book aside and left the living-room. The ghost followed her upstairs, to the front bedroom. There was an older woman lying in the bed.

Julie smiled at her. "How are you, Mam? Is there anything I can get you?"

Mrs Logan smiled weakly and shook her head. "Stay with me, love, for a few minutes."

The ghost watched as Julie took the old woman's hand and sat by the bed.

"The doctor says Dad's going to be fine," Julie said, trying to put on a brave smile. "He should be home in a few days."

Mrs Logan nodded. "I know, I know."

The ghost watched the older Julie and her mother for most of the day, but gradually it realised that there was nothing to be learned here but the fact that Julie was alive.

It returned to what it thought of as its own time, with Julie and Brian. It wondered at the reason for its journey. Why did my future self tell me to go there? Was there some clue that I will need?

* * *

Mrs Prentiss came back to the house at three o'clock. She was full of chat and ready for a good long talk with Julie, but she went straight to work when she noticed that Grandad Tom was in the house.

She was beginning to wonder if she'd ever get a chance to ask Julie about Father McCanney, when she answered a knock at the front door to find the young priest himself standing there.

"Good afternoon, Mrs Prentiss. Is Mr Kavanagh home? I'd like to have a word with him, if I may."

"Certainly, Father. Come in." She led the priest into the living-room, where Tom was sitting at his desk.

"Father McCanney, how are you?" Tom said, rising from his chair and offering his hand to the priest. "Mrs Prentiss, would you be a dear and bring us some tea?"

Mrs Prentiss nodded politely and left the room, quietly muttering about slavery.

Father McCanney smiled cheerfully. "So, have you had any more trouble with your ghost, Mr Kavanagh?"

Tom laughed. "Why do you ask? I thought yesterday that you didn't really believe me."

"Yesterday I *didn't* believe you. Today I'm not so convinced of the impossibility of it at all." He took a deep breath, and continued. "Last night I was thinking about your ghost. I was wondering why it might be stuck here on earth, rather than moving on to the next world. I remember wondering where it might be destined, Heaven or Hell. I was writing in my notebook at the time, and I think I have an answer." He reached into his pocket and removed a folded sheet of lined paper. He passed it to Tom.

"Before I look at this, Father, I must ask you if you've shown it to anyone else."

"No one. I paid a visit to the archbishop this morning, but he was too busy to see me."

"I see." Tom unfolded the sheet of paper and read it. "Good lord! This can't be right! This wasn't what I wrote earlier."

Father McCanney was surprised. "Earlier? What do you mean?"

They were interrupted by Mrs Prentiss arriving with a tray laden with tea and biscuits. She left it on the desk, said "Don't mention it" when they took no notice of her, and left. She paused to curtsy at the door, but they didn't notice that either.

"Have a look at this." Tom opened his journal and showed it to the priest. "Something seemed to take control of my hand earlier. This is what it wrote."

"'Help Me'. I see. When it took control of *my* hand last night, I managed to stop it by grabbing the pencil with my teeth. That would explain the bottom part of the second 'L' – the pencil dragged across the page as I was trying to get control of it. It must have been trying to write a 'P', but I stopped it halfway. I must admit, seeing the whole message makes me feel a lot better about your ghost."

"So you believe in the ghost now, Father McCanney?"

The priest nodded. "I do. I've never experienced anything like this before. Not counting hypnotism, it defies all logical explanation, and I doubt if I was hypnotised. I'm sorry I didn't believe you before, but there was no proof."

"The Lord says 'Blessed are those who have not seen, and yet believe.' Something I've heard you tell the parishioners on more than one occasion, Father."

The priest reached across the desk and took back the page from his notebook. "Has anything else happened, Mr Kavanagh?"

"Yes, Brian and Julie both saw the ghost, on separate occasions. They are the first to actually see it. Whatever it is, it's getting more desperate," Tom said.

117

"Why do you say that?"

"Father McCanney, you don't think it's just here for no reason, do you? No, the ghost has a purpose, and from what we can tell, it needs our help."

"But how? What could we possibly do to help it?"

"I wish I knew, Father. I wish I knew. There's something else, though. Julie and Brian feel that the ghost is my mother. I still have my doubts, but they're convinced."

"I see. When did your mother die?"

"In 1943. She was fifty-five. She had a heart attack."

"But you don't think it's her?"

Tom shrugged. "I don't know. The ghost has been around for a long time, since long before 1943."

"Well, is there anyone else who it could be?"

"I don't know. Brian made the point that a ghost wouldn't necessarily be affected by time the way we are, so there's nothing to stop it from visiting the future or the past."

Father McCanney paused thoughtfully. "I'll tell you what I'll do, Mr Kavanagh, I'll check up the old parish records for this house and the surrounding land. Perhaps something of relevance might turn up. It could be the ghost of someone who died centuries ago."

"Then why would it look like my mother?" Tom asked.

"Perhaps it assumes a shape that is recognisable to the people around it."

Tom sighed. "You could be right. But it's been much more active since Julie and Brian came . . . why would it be connected with them?"

"I don't know. I might be inclined to think it's a

118

poltergeist . . . they're apparently attracted to young teenagers, but to be honest, I doubt that's what it is." The priest stood up. "I have to go, Mr Kavanagh, I'm taking the evening service for Father Mitchell. If anything happens, please let me know. This is very important to me."

"Thank you, Father. I'll phone if anything happens." Tom pushed himself up out of his chair. "I'll walk you to the gate."

* * *

Mrs Prentiss watched Tom and Father McCanney walk down the drive, then went into the living-room to collect the tray. She was disgusted that they'd left the tea to grow cold and hadn't even touched the biscuits. She picked up the tray, turned around to leave, and screamed.

The tray crashed to the floor, spilling the lukewarm tea over the carpet.

119

CHAPTER FOURTEEN

Mrs Prentiss sat shaking in the kitchen. Tom, Julie and Brian sat with her, trying to convince her that the ghost wasn't dangerous.

"It scared the *life* out of me!" Mrs Prentiss said. "It was horrible, I've never seen anything like it."

"We think it's the ghost of Grandad's mother," Julie said softly, trying to console the older woman.

"It could be, I don't know. That doesn't make things any better," Mrs Prentiss said. She took a deep breath and sipped at the brandy that Tom had given her to help calm her nerves. "I'm sorry, Mr Kavanagh, but I don't think I can continue working for you."

Tom was shocked. "But Mrs Prentiss, the ghost doesn't do any harm. In fact, it needs us to free it, to let it go on to the next world."

"I don't care. Look at it from my point of view – I don't really need this job, and you're certainly not paying me enough to put up with something like *that*," she said, gesturing towards the living-room. She knocked back the rest of the brandy and stood up. "I've got to go."

120

Tom followed her to the kitchen door. "Go, if you feel that you must, Mrs Prentiss, but remember that the job will always be open for you."

She looked back at Julie and Brian. "I'm sorry."

"There is one more thing," Tom said. "Please don't mention this to anyone. It would only make things worse."

"People are going to wonder why I left after all this time, Mr Kavanagh."

Tom nodded and thought for a few moments. "Tell them I've given you three weeks off, seeing as Brian and Julie are here. Paid holiday, of course."

Mrs Prentiss sighed. "You're bribing me, Mr Kavanagh."

Tom started to deny it, but then he realised she was right. He nodded. "Yes. I'm bribing you not to mention this to anyone else. Look, Mrs Prentiss, we think we've made a breakthrough in discovering the nature of the ghost. With any luck it'll all be over within three weeks. If that happens, will you consider coming back?"

"I'll consider it. Goodbye, Mr Kavanagh." She opened the front door and left.

Tom came back into the kitchen. "Well, at least we know we're all not imagining things."

"Do you trust her not to talk, Grandad?" Julie asked.

"I don't know. Mrs Prentiss has a good heart, but she does tend to indulge in gossip a bit too much for my liking."

"So what do we do now?" Brian asked.

His grandfather shrugged. "That's up to the ghost."

* * *

The rest of the day passed quietly. Julie and Brian studied some more while their grandfather read through his journal, hoping to find some clue to help them.

In the afternoon of the following day, Wednesday, Julie asked her grandfather about the upcoming summer festival.

"Oh yes, it's been running every year for as long as I can remember. Two weeks of exactly the same things as every other day of the year, only with bunting."

"So it's not going to be much fun, then?"

"Oh, well, now . . . you see that depends on . . . I mean, if you're young, like you are, then there's . . ." He smiled. "No, it'll be as awful as every other year. Sorry, love."

"I heard that there's a disco on in the school tomorrow night. Do you mind if I go along?"

"What time does it end at?"

Julie shrugged. "I don't know. It starts at eight, so I suppose it won't be over until after eleven. Is that okay?"

"How will you get home? The school is nearly a mile and a half away."

"Well, I'll walk, I suppose."

He shook his head slowly. "No, I don't think so. Not on your own. If Brian was with you, that'd be different."

"Okay, thanks anyway," Julie said as she left the room.

She went up to her bedroom and sat down on the bed, thinking about the problem.

She didn't want Brian to go to the disco with her, because then he'd find out about Phil, but her grandfather wouldn't let her go without Brian. And she couldn't go with both Brian and Phil anyway, as there were only two tickets. How am I going to work this out? she asked herself. I can't just tell Phil I'm not able to make it, and I'm certainly not going to just stand him up. There was one obvious solution; she could tell her grandfather that Phil had asked her out. That way Phil could walk her home and there was no need for Brian to be involved at all. Maybe that'll be the best, Julie thought. After all, I don't want to have to lie to Grandad. And I'm not just going to sneak out.

But what will I do about Brian? It's not really fair to leave him behind, but there are only two tickets.

She took the tickets out of her purse. They had the word "Complimentary" stamped on them, but underneath that was a price of two pounds fifty. Well, Brian can certainly afford that. He can pay to get in.

And then Brian will find out about Phil. She sighed. But why shouldn't he? She asked herself. There's no crime in going out with someone. It's nothing to be ashamed of. Why shouldn't Brian know about Phil? Because he'll make fun of me.

So let him.

* * *

After dinner, Julie told her grandfather that a boy in the town had asked her out.

Grandad Tom looked up from his newspaper. "Has he, indeed? Do you know him?"

"Well, I do now. I've met him a couple of times. He's really nice."

123

He smiled. "They all are, dear, at first."

"I asked Mrs Prentiss about him, she says that he's okay."

"And I presume that he's the one who asked you to the disco?"

Julie nodded.

"What's this lad's name then?"

"Philip Hudson. His mother owns the chemist's."

"Mrs Hudson's lad, eh? Well, if Mrs Prentiss approves, I suppose I shouldn't stop you. But be home by eleven at the latest. And I don't care if they start playing your favourite song just as you walk out the door. Eleven o'clock, understood?"

Julie grinned. "Thanks, Grandad!"

"And make sure he walks you right up to the door. It's a long way up from the gate, you never know who might be hiding in the bushes."

"Well, after all that's happened with the ghost and everything, I'm not going to be frightened by a mugger or a burglar or anything like that," Julie said.

Grandad Tom closed his newspaper, folded it, and took off his glasses. "So, are you going to ask Brian if he wants to go along?"

"Aw, Grandad, he'll ruin everything!"

"Yes, I suppose he probably will."

"Anyway, he fell out of the tree on Sunday. He's not supposed to be doing too much; the doctor said he was to take it easy. And he'd probably have a rotten time and I imagine that he hates discos. *And* I've been stuck with him day and night for nearly two weeks."

Julie's grandfather smiled at her. "Well, that sounds like perfectly logical reasoning if ever I heard it."

She ignored his sarcasm. "This is the first time that anyone's ever asked me out, Grandad! I don't want anything to spoil it."

He put up his hands in defence. "All right, all right! There's usually more than one thing on at a time during the festival. I'll go along to something myself, and I'll bring Brian with me. I imagine that there'll be a slide show about flower arranging, or something incredibly boring like that."

Julie hugged him. "Thanks, Grandad! You're great!"

* * *

Father Peter McCanney sat at a desk in the library. In front of him was a pile of ancient, dusty leather-bound books: the history of the parish going back to the sixteenth century.

The priest had always been fascinated with Irish history, and he found himself continually distracted by pieces of information that had nothing to do with Tom Kavanagh's house or the land on which it lay.

The earliest local newspaper that he had found was dated Friday, the eighth of August, 1902. Its yellowing pages had been sealed in plastic, and the librarian had made him promise he wouldn't remove it from the library. The newspaper was appropriately entitled *The News*. It was only eight pages long and there was little of interest in it. Most of the news concerned deaths and births. There was no mention of politics, and Father McCanney had to continually remind himself that at that time Ireland had been under British rule.

The masthead of the newspaper said that it was

written and published by Hubert James Peterson, a local landlord. On an impulse, the priest opened a book listing important local figures, and searched for an entry on Peterson. The book had been printed in 1910, but was in remarkably fine condition. After reading the introduction and a few of the entries, Father McCanney realised why the book was in such good shape: It was very, very dull.

The entry on Peterson spanned more than seven pages, all printed in a very small type-face. Seeing this, Father McCanney groaned. He read the first paragraph.

"Peterson, Hubert James, MD. Born London, 1852. Although at first a promising student of architecture, Peterson felt compelled to study medicine, and received his Doctorate of Medicine from Cambridge in 1883. Peterson's family once owned all of the land on which the town now stands, but when his father (John O'Neill Peterson, see entry on same) passed on in 1895, Peterson continued his father's tradition of systematically dividing up the land and awarding it to hardworking locals."

Father McCanney skimmed over the next couple of pages. This book, he said to himself, is probably the most wildly inaccurate piece of history I've ever read. He flicked to the printing details at the start of the book, and laughed out loud when he read "Printed and bound by Peterson Publishing, London." On the inside front cover was a note to the effect that the book had kindly been donated to the library by Hubert Peterson's son.

The priest rubbed his eyes and stretched. The library was about to close. He asked the librarian if he could photocopy some excerpts from the books. When she agreed, he chose some pages randomly and copied them.

He walked home with a bundle of pages and the few books he'd been allowed to borrow tucked under his arm. There must be something in here that will help, he said to himself. Something that will give us a way to get rid of the ghost, whatever it is.

* * *

The ghost knew who she was. It had taken her a long time but, with the clues supplied by Julie and Brian, she finally realised her identity.

But how did I come to be in this state, and why am I here? Why did I not pass on to the next world?

When Ciarán Kavanagh died, she hadn't seen his spirit rising from his body. Does that mean that a ghost is not just a disembodied soul? Is it possible that I am something different? I must let the children know, they may be able to help me.

She drifted across the winds of time, allowing herself to be dragged into those periods where the emotion was strongest. She found herself once again in the empty house.

Standing before her was her earlier self.

"You are my future," the other ghost said. "You cannot be my past, as I do not remember a meeting like this before."

She nodded. "I am your future. I remember this encounter, from your point of view." Even though she remembered saying the words the other ghost had just said, and she remembered hearing the answer, it seemed perfectly natural to respond the same way.

127

"Will they succeed?" The other ghost's face looked worried.

She smiled at the idea of a ghost fretting about a living person. "Yes. They are very close, success is only days away. But there is still danger."

"Danger? To the children?"

"And to you. Beware the young priest. His intentions are good, but he can cause much pain. You must guide him. Also, watch the boy Philip Hudson. He is a distraction to Julie. She is the one you need." She didn't understand the reference to guiding the priest, but she remembered hearing that from her future self, and she knew it must be important.

"But if there is danger, and you have warned me of it, does that not change things?"

She smiled again. This conversation was much less worrying from this point of view. "No. You see, I was warned of it too."

"Why are you here? Why did you locate me? Was it just to give me riddles?"

"I too remember asking that. I am here to help you, but I can tell you only one more thing."

"And what is that?"

She began to fade, not wanting the other ghost to ask too many questions. "Go further. Much further. At least twenty years . . . you will see. You will see . . ."

CHAPTER FIFTEEN

On Thursday afternoon Brian and his grandfather found themselves arguing in the living-room.

"I'd much rather go to the disco, Grandad," Brian said.

"No, you wouldn't," his grandfather replied. "Discos are boring and full of tedious people."

Brian sighed. There seemed to be no getting around the old man. "Aw, come on, Grandad! You're letting Julie go!"

Grandad Tom looked at him sternly. "So? You don't think that's fair?"

"No, I don't."

Tom shrugged. "Sometimes life is unfair. Brian, Julie's been stuck here with you for nearly two weeks. Don't you think it's time she had a night off?"

"That's not the point."

"Yes it is. Look, it's not that she doesn't want you to go along, I just think that she should have some time to herself."

"You're actually letting her go to a disco all by herself?"

"She's not going by herself. She's going with a friend of hers who lives in the village. There'll be another disco before the festival is over. You can go along to that one instead. Anyway, you'll enjoy tonight's lecture a lot more than the disco."

Brian scowled. "*Enjoy* a lecture on antique cars? I doubt it."

His grandfather grinned. "Want to place a little bet on it?"

Brian couldn't believe what he'd heard. "A *bet*? You're kidding!"

Grandad Tom took out his wallet and removed a crisp five-pound note. "This fiver says that you'll enjoy the lecture a lot more than the disco."

Brian was stunned into silence. When he finally recovered, he dug into his pocket and pulled out a handful of pound coins. He counted out five and placed them on the mantelpiece. "It's a bet." His grandfather placed his money beside it. They shook hands.

"Remember," Grandad Tom said, "it's considered extremely bad form to back out of a bet."

Brian grinned. "Don't worry, *I've* no intention of backing out!" He rubbed his hands together. This is great, he said to himself. This will be the easiest five quid I've ever made! And all I have to do is have a rotten time. Not that that'll be too hard, he added.

* * *

Julie climbed out of the bath at five-thirty, then spent the next hour getting ready.

Should I wear something casual, she wondered, or

130

something sophisticated? She looked at her collection of clothes spread out on the bed, and sighed. Something sophisticated among this lot? What a joke.

Eventually, after various combinations of most of her clothes, Julie decided on brown slacks and a tan blouse. She was pleased with her reflection in the mirror; the clothes went well with her brown eyes and dark blonde hair.

Since this was a special occasion she took a gold chain from her small jewellery box. It had been a present from her parents the previous Christmas, and she was terrified of losing it. It had a tiny gold-plated "J" strung on an incredibly fine chain.

At a quarter past six Julie began to wonder if she should wear any make-up. By half-past six, she'd become extremely worried about it. *What if he doesn't like me with make-up? What if he doesn't even recognise me? What if it rains on the way to his house and the make-up runs?*

Should I bring my jacket in case it does *rain? And if I do, where will I leave it? I can't go on to the dance floor carrying a jacket, but someone might steal it. Mam would go mad.*

At a quarter to seven, Julie was panicking over which shoes to wear. Her runners didn't go with her blouse and trousers. She had a pair of black shoes with tiny heels, but they were very uncomfortable and she hated wearing them.

She was standing on her bed, wearing her left shoe and her right runner, and trying to see which looked best in the mirror, when there was a knock on her bedroom door.

"Julie? Are you decent?" It was Brian.

"Hang on!" She got down off the bed and opened the door.

"I was just wondering," Brian said, "if you need any money for tonight."

Julie gasped. In all the excitement, she'd completely forgotten that she'd almost no money with her. "I meant to go to the bank machine today, but I never thought of it! Brian, could you . . .?"

"Sure," he said, grinning. He reached into his pocket and took out a ten-pound note.

"Thanks! I'll pay you back sometime."

"It's okay, keep it."

Julie smiled at him. "You're great! Thanks again."

"No problem. Have a good time." Brian turned to leave, but Julie grabbed his arm.

"Well?" she said.

"Well what?"

"I've spent ages getting ready. How do I look?"

He grinned. "You mean apart from the odd shoes? Yeah, you look okay."

Julie took off her shoe and runner. "Only okay?"

"What do you expect me to say? Don't worry, I think your friend will approve."

"Oh. Grandad told you then?"

"I sort of guessed that you weren't going alone," Brian said. "About this friend of yours; do you think she'd like *me*?"

Julie bit her lip to stop herself from laughing. She shook her head. "I don't think so, Brian. I don't think you're really my friend's type."

Brian shrugged. "Never mind. I was just curious. Have a good time anyway."

"Thanks, I'll try."

Julie closed the door and burst out laughing.

* * *

By drifting back and forth through time, the ghost had managed to piece together the events leading up to her death.

She knew at last why she had been trapped, not allowed to go on to the next world, and she was worried.

When Ciarán Kavanagh died, I didn't see his spirit. When Tom's baby sister died, there was no sign of anything like me. But I exist. Perhaps it is different when someone is born . . . Does the soul enter the body at birth, or before?

She decided to visit the time of Julie's birth. The hospital was bright and noisy, and packed with people even though it was ten o'clock at night. Seán Logan, Julie's father, was waiting outside the delivery room. The ghost watched him for a while, smiling at his nervousness.

The ghost faded and reappeared inside the delivery room. The nurse told Susan Logan to push one final time, and the baby was born.

She felt a tremendous rush of emotion. This is what life is about: the cry of a new-born child.

Then she felt sad. There is so much for this girl to do. Her life will be so full. The ghost allowed herself to return to the house. Julie's grandfather was reading in bed and Mrs Prentiss was asleep in a chair in the front bedroom. As the ghost watched, the housekeeper jerked

*awake, then looked at her watch. She went downstairs
and phoned the hospital.*

*The ghost watched Mrs Prentiss cry with happiness
when she heard the news.*

* * *

Father McCanney had discovered something startling
among the books he'd borrowed from the library.

In 1745 an old woman had been beaten to death as
she slept in her cottage. Many of the people from the
local village had believed she was a witch, and one night
a group of drunk young men had managed to convince
themselves that the old woman was the cause of
numerous recent misfortunes, including the deaths of
three cows on a nearby farm and the drowning of a
toddler in a local well.

The young men – the toddler's father among them –
stormed the old woman's cottage and clubbed her to
death. And although everyone knew who they had been,
the men had never been brought to justice.

Father McCanney searched through the rest of the
books for another mention of the incident, and found a
reference listing the men believed to have been
involved. The priest had assumed that there might be an
ancestor of Tom Kavanagh's among the killers, but none
of their surnames had been Kavanagh. One of them,
however, was Peterson.

James Peterson was the son of the landlord at the
time. He'd been accustomed to drinking with the men
from the village, and Father McCanney guessed that if

Peterson had been involved his family would have wanted the matter covered up.

It was as he was looking through the crude maps of the period that the priest realised that Tom Kavanagh's house was built almost exactly on the site of the old woman's cottage. Father McCanney nodded to himself. And it was Peterson's descendant, Hubert James, who built the house; It's no wonder that her ghost has been left behind. She's trying to get revenge on Peterson's family. It's Tom Kavanagh's bad luck that the house was built where it is.

He went down to the hall and phoned Tom's house. He let it ring for almost five minutes, but there was no answer.

He went back up to his room, knelt before the crucifix and prayed for guidance. As he prayed, his gaze fell upon the two white candles he kept on the windowsill in case of a power failure.

Father McCanney looked at his watch. It was only seven-thirty. I'll phone again in an hour, then another hour after that. If there's still no sign of them, I'll go up to the house.

* * *

At exactly seven-thirty, Julie found herself outside the chemist's, her jacket rolled up and tucked under one arm. The shutters were down, so she walked to the door on their left and rang the bell.

A middle-aged man leaned out of the upstairs window. "Yes?"

Julie was so nervous she could barely speak. "Em . . . I'm looking for Phil."

The man chuckled. "You've got the wrong house, love. It's the door on the other side."

Julie blushed. "Thanks."

"Not at all." Still chuckling, he pulled himself back in and closed the window.

Julie walked to the door on the right of the shutters. As she reached it the door opened and Phil stepped out. "Hi! I see you met Mister Ferguson."

She blushed even more and buried her face in her hands. "Oh God! This is so embarrassing!"

"Don't worry, he's all right, he won't tell anyone."

Julie smiled at him. Phil was wearing a white T-shirt and a pair of jeans. "Uh oh," Julie said. "I hope I'm not overdressed for this."

Phil looked her up and down. "No! You look great! All my mates will be dead jealous."

"All your mates? Oh no!"

Phil pulled the door closed behind him. "Ready?"

She nodded. "I've got the tickets here."

"Great. I was thinking we could take the car, but it's such a nice night, we might as well walk."

"You can drive?"

"Sure. But Mam doesn't let me use the car too often."

They walked part of the way in silence. Julie couldn't think of anything to talk about, she was too worried about meeting Phil's friends. "Phil? What you said about your friends being at the disco . . . you weren't serious, were you?"

"Oh, there won't be any of my friends at the disco.

At least, I don't think so. But you know how things are – people will talk."

"So you're not ashamed to be seen with me, then?"

He laughed. "Ashamed? Don't be daft. I'm proud." He put his arm around Julie's waist.

Julie smiled. Maireád can *keep* Craig Kipling, she said to herself.

* * *

The lecture on antique cars wasn't as dull as Brian had imagined it would be, but he pretended to be bored for the sake of his five pounds. He became particularly interested when the lecturer mentioned the use of computer-aided technology in restoring the cars, but he whispered to his grandfather that the lecturer had found the single most unimaginative use for a computer.

"Don't even bother trying," Grandad Tom whispered back. "That fiver is as good as mine."

Brian returned his attention to the lecture. Maybe Grandad knows something I don't, he said to himself. Maybe this *will* get interesting. He listened for a few minutes.

" . . . and when the synchromesh has been disengaged, the collar and gear wheel are of course then not connected and the gear wheel is allowed to freewheel on the transmission shaft. With the aid of the computer, the alignment can be optimised to provide more accurate . . ."

Of course, Brian thought as the words went over his head, Grandad could be having me on.

* * *

At eight-thirty, Father McCanney phoned the house again. There was no answer. He picked up his candles from the windowsill and blessed them. Then he removed the crucifix from the wall and put it in his bag, along with the candles, three bottles he'd filled with holy water from the font in the church and a small tin box containing the consecrated host.

He blessed himself. "Help me, Lord. I don't know if I can do this. I hope I don't have to."

He opened his Bible and began to read, occasionally glancing at his watch as the hands crawled slowly round to nine-thirty.

CHAPTER SIXTEEN

The disco was held in the secondary school's gymnasium. Balloons and streamers had been tied to the climbing bars against one of the walls, and various other hastily-arranged decorations were taped to the other walls and the ceiling. The disc jockey was well past middle-age, and insisted on playing only songs from the sixties and seventies. The only refreshment available came in the form of small plastic cups of Fanta which, at fifty pence each, Julie considered to be a complete waste of money. There were less than forty people of Julie's age at the disco, who were doing their best to enjoy themselves despite the presence of some of the town's older folk and a small group of surly teachers acting as watchdogs in case anyone seemed to be enjoying themselves *too* much.

Just before nine o'clock, when "Shake, Rattle and Roll" was on its third outing on the ancient, scratchy record deck, Julie and Phil decided they'd had enough.

Julie handed in her cloakroom ticket to a nasty old woman who eyed them suspiciously and asked why they were leaving so early.

"Oh, I've had a brilliant time," Julie lied. "But I said I'd be home by half nine, and I don't want to be late."

This show of apparent juvenile obedience brightened up the old bat, who handed Julie her jacket, gave her a cheery wave and told her she must come to the end-of-festival disco, where she was bound to have an even better time.

"God, I'm glad that's over," Julie said as they left the school's lobby.

Phil took her hand as they walked. "I'm sorry it wasn't great. Now you know why I hate discos."

"Haven't you ever been to a real disco?"

"No. And I don't think I want to go to one either."

"Well, they aren't all as bad as that one was. Is it like that every year?"

Phil shook his head. "Not at all. Sometimes it's really, *really* awful."

Julie laughed. "Maybe you should have gone to the cinema after all."

"There's always tomorrow night. Would you like to come along?"

"Well, I'll have to ask my Grandad, but I'm sure it'll be okay."

"Do you want to hear a great knock-knock joke?" Phil asked.

Julie shrugged. "Okay."

"Right, you start it."

"Knock knock."

Phil grinned. "Who's there?"

Julie started to answer, but then realised that she'd been well and truly caught out. "That's a rotten trick! Well, where I come from, we have a different sort of knock-knock joke, called a knick-knock joke."

"A *knick-knock* joke? Let's hear one."

"Knick knock."

"Who's there?"

Julie didn't answer.

"I said who's there?"

She still didn't answer.

Phil frowned. "I don't get it."

"There's no one there. It's a knick-knock! You know, ringing the bell and running away. My friend Simone told me that one."

Phil groaned. "That's terrible! I thought *my* jokes were bad."

"Oh, they are, believe me."

"Okay," Phil said. "What do you get if you cross the Atlantic ocean with an elephant?"

"I don't know."

"Wet."

It was Julie's turn to groan. "All right, why does Noddy have big ears? No, wait a minute, I got that wrong."

Phil laughed. "It's okay, I heard it before. You'll like this one. There's this guy, right, and he loves seafood. Every week he goes into the same seafood restaurant because he knows the waiter, a foreign guy called Yuface. And one day he decides to have squid –"

"Uh oh," Julie said. "It's not that old 'here's the sick squid I owe you' joke, is it?"

"No, it's much better than that. Where was I?"

"In a restaurant."

"Yeah, thanks. Now, all the fish and things are in a big tank, and the waiter takes them out and brings them to the chef, who kills and cooks them. So he tells Yuface that he wants squid, and Yuface says 'Do you want green squid or brown?'. So the guy says 'Green'. Then Yuface says 'Do you want tame or wild squid?' The guy chooses wild. Next the waiter asks him 'Do you want squid with ordinary lips or hairy lips?' So he chooses one with hairy lips."

"Squid don't have lips," Julie said.

"They do in this joke. Anyway, Yuface gets the squid and brings it into the kitchen, but he can't bring himself to kill it. So he asks Hans, the guy who washes up, to kill the squid. But Hans can't do it either. And the moral of the story is –"

Julie interrupted him. "Hans that does dishes can be soft as Yuface with wild green hairy-lipped squid."

"You heard it before! Why didn't you stop me? I could have saved a lot of energy!"

Julie grinned. "Oh, but you tell it so well."

Phil looked at his watch. "It's nearly half-nine. Do you want to go straight home, or should we go somewhere else?"

"Are you hungry?" Julie asked. Phil nodded. "Great," she said. "Come back to the house. I'll make us something to eat."

* * *

They met Father McCanney on the way to the house. He seemed extremely relieved to meet Julie. "I tried phoning your grandad," he said. "There was no answer. Do you know if he's gone out?"

"He has. He brought Brian to a lecture on antique cars."

"Ah, well, that's okay then." He looked awkwardly at them for a few seconds.

"Do you want me to tell him you're looking for him?" Julie asked.

"Do, please. Can you ask him to phone me as soon as he gets in?"

"Sure. Is everything all right?"

It seemed to Julie that the priest had something on his mind. "What? Oh, everything's fine. Never mind." He said goodbye and turned in the direction of the town, away from Tom Kavanagh's house.

Phil turned to Julie. "Is there something going on that I should know about?"

Julie tried to look as innocent as possible. "No, nothing."

Phil hummed to himself. "Well, then. Is there something going on that I *shouldn't* know about?"

Julie just laughed and ran ahead. "I'll race you to the gate!"

"You're on!"

She kept running. When she looked back, Phil was far behind and labouring to catch up. Julie pretended to be winded, and stopped against the wall.

When Phil finally caught up with her, he said "You're pretty fast."

"Only over short distances. Anyway, I had a head start. Come on, we'll take it easy from here."

They walked hand in hand to the gate of her grandfather's house. "It's not as big as I thought it was," Phil said, looking up at the house. "The way everyone talks you'd think that your grandad lives in a mansion."

"Well, it's more than big enough for only one person."

"Who's staying here at the moment?"

"Just me, Brian and Grandad."

"Oh." Phil pointed to an upstairs window. "So who's that, then?"

Julie looked up to where he was pointing. She could see a vague, hazy figure looking out of the front bedroom window.

She stood looking for several seconds, then grabbed Phil's hand and pulled him away. "Come on, there's this really great tree around the back. You just have to see it."

"Okay, I'm coming." Phil took a last look at the figure in the window, and allowed Julie to drag him around the side of the house.

* * *

In the back garden, Julie enthused at length about the fun she'd had there when she was a child. She tried to be cheerful and natural, but she knew it sounded forced. Gradually, she calmed down and began to cry.

Phil put his arms around her and hugged her. "It's okay, it's all right."

Julie sobbed. "It's not all right. Things are just getting worse and worse, and there's nothing we can do to stop it."

"Stop what?" Phil asked. He stroked her hair. "Tell me about it, Julie."

She stepped back and shook her head. "No, you wouldn't believe me."

Phil handed her his handkerchief, and she wiped her eyes on it.

144

"Who was that woman in the window?" Phil asked. His voice was gentle and caring, and Julie started to cry again.

Phil took her hand and led her to the garden bench. They sat down, and Phil put his arm around Julie's shoulders.

Julie sniffed. "Do you remember on Tuesday, in the café, when I asked you if you believed in ghosts?"

Phil nodded. "Yes, I remember. Are you telling me that the woman in the window is a ghost?"

"I *said* you wouldn't believe me."

"I'm not saying I don't believe you. Tell me all about it."

* * *

Phil stood up and stretched. He hadn't realised how tense he'd become listening to Julie's story. "But you've no real proof of any of this?"

"No, only what we've seen and heard," Julie said. "Oh! There's the writing, of course."

"In your grandad's journal. Can I have a look at it?"

Julie nodded and stood up. They walked around to the front of the house, and Phil looked up to see if there was anyone in the window.

"She won't be there," Julie said. "She only appears about once a day."

"Yes, so far. But you said you think it's getting stronger. Aren't you afraid?"

Julie opened the hall door and looked back at him. "I'm terrified, but somehow I feel she's not going to harm any of us. We have to try to help her."

They walked into the house and Julie showed her Grandfather's journal to Phil. He flicked through the pages, reading short pieces here and there, and stopped when he saw the words "Help me" scrawled on the page. "This is it?" He asked.

Julie nodded. "Grandad said it's the same thing Father McCanney wrote, except that *he* didn't get to finish it. What do you think?"

"I don't know. Mass hysteria doesn't seem likely, and I doubt you're all doing this as part of some obscure joke. I definitely saw someone at the window."

"So, do you believe me?" Julie watched Phil's face anxiously, searching for some sign that he thought she was mad, but he just smiled and nodded thoughtfully.

"Yes, I believe you."

* * *

Brian and his grandfather walked home slowly. Brian put on a big show as to how much he hadn't enjoyed the lecture, but Grandad Tom just smiled and nodded as he listened to him.

"So," Grandad Tom said, "On a scale of one to ten, how did the lecture rate?"

Brian hummed and tutted for a moment. "Well, I'll be generous, and give it two out of ten."

"Two? As much as that? Well, well, well. So, on a scale of one to ten, how much did you enjoy the disco?"

"What? But I didn't *go* to the disco!"

"So you couldn't have enjoyed it at all, then."

"No way! You're trying to cheat me out of my five quid!"

His grandfather chuckled. "What exactly did we bet on, then?"

"That I'd enjoy the lecture more than the disco, but you meant that I'd enjoy the lecture more than the disco if I'd gone to it."

"Now, I don't remember what we meant, only what we said. And you didn't enjoy the disco at all, so therefore I win the bet."

Brian was raging. "That's a rotten trick and you know it!"

"Tough. You really didn't think I'd let you win a fiver off me, did you? I mean, did you really imagine that your old grandad was daft enough to fall for that?"

"Well, this isn't fair!"

"I'll tell you what, though, I'll cancel the bet if you cut the grass in the morning."

"This is what you had in mind all along, isn't it?"

"Yep. Well, what do you say?"

Brian grinned. "Okay, I agree. I'll cut the grass in the morning."

His grandfather patted him on the shoulder. "Good lad. And by that I mean *all* of the grass, not just one blade. You weren't thinking of something like that, were you?"

"Of course not, Grandad," Brian lied. "I wouldn't try to trick a member of my own family. Unlike some people."

They had reached the gate of the house. Grandad Tom pointed at the garden with his umbrella. "Over there, all of that between the bushes and the flower-beds. And round the back, of course. And remember the agreement? I said cut the grass in the morning, that

147

means before noon, so don't let me catch you skiving off."

Brian groaned. "I've changed my mind. You can keep the fiver."

"You've changed you mind? Well, I haven't changed *mine*. You cut the grass in the morning, and no complaints, right?"

Brian sighed. "Yes, Grandad."

Grandad Tom opened the door. Inside, they could hear Julie talking to someone. Brian was surprised, but his grandfather just whispered, "It's okay, it's probably Julie's young man."

"Young man?" Brian whispered back. "So *that's* why you didn't want me to go to the disco!"

Tom slammed the hall door loudly. "We're home! Anybody in?" He winked slyly at Brian.

Julie opened the living-room door. "Phil's here." She looked sternly at them. "I told him about the ghost."

"Indeed? And does he believe you?"

"Come in and talk to him, Grandad. See for yourself."

* * *

The four of them talked for nearly an hour. Phil spent most of the time listening, asking only occasional questions. When they'd finished, he nodded, then stood and began pacing the room.

"Well, I know you're not all lying. I saw something myself, so I know it exists." He turned to Brian. "What you said about the ghost not being fixed in time makes a lot of sense. At least, as much sense as the rest of this makes. But two questions remain. First, why is the ghost here?" He looked around at the others, but they all shrugged.

"The second question is more important," Phil said. "Exactly who is the ghost?"

"I thought we'd covered that," Brian said. "We think it's Grandad's mother. Our great-grandmother."

Phil shook his head. "I don't think so. It doesn't fit in with everything else."

"Like what?" Brian asked.

"Like why she's here now. What good could she achieve? Anyway, I'm not the only one who doubts that it's your grandad's mother. Father McCanney seems to think it's something much worse."

"Why do you say that?" Grandad Tom asked.

"Oh! I forgot," Julie said. "We met him earlier, Grandad. He wanted you to ring him as soon as you got in. Sorry, I never thought of it."

Her grandfather looked at his watch. "Well, it's too late to ring him now. I'll do it in the morning."

They talked for a few minutes more, but this time Julie was silent. Eventually, she jumped up. "I've just thought of something! Oh, my God!" She put her hand to her mouth and looked as though she was about to faint.

Phil caught her, and helped her sit back down. "What is it?"

"Oh, God! I hope I'm wrong!"

Phil held her hand. "Tell us, Julie. What is it?"

She shook her head slowly, trying not to believe her thoughts. "What Brian said about the ghost . . . that she's not fixed in time. She can go where and when she wants to. The past, or the future, remember?" Julie shivered. "If the ghost can visit the past, who's to say she's not doing that when *we* see her?

"The ghost could be someone who hasn't died yet!"

149

CHAPTER SEVENTEEN

Seán Logan walked out to his wife, who was sitting on the edge of the swimming-pool, staring vacantly into the water. He sat down beside her and put his arm around her shoulder.

"Cheer up, love. It was too good to be true."

Susan gave him a brave smile and nodded. "You're right, I suppose. A week in Spain is better then nothing."

"Don't be too hard on him, Sue. It's not Billy's fault he's an idiot."

She sighed, and kicked at the water. "It's probably just as well that Julie's not here. She'd have told him what she thought of him. I nearly did myself."

"I suppose he phoned the other couple?"

Susan nodded. "Yeah. They're flying in tomorrow. They refused to cancel. I don't blame them, it's Billy's fault for getting the dates wrong."

"That's the trouble with a time-share place, you could arrive to find someone else already there. When we're rich, love, we'll buy our own place."

Susan scooped up a handful of water and threw it at him. "You're a dreamer, Seán Logan! I don't know why I ever married you!" She laughed.

"Because you loved me," Seán said. "I hope you still do."

"Of course I do. Come here." Susan put her arms around her husband and hugged him, then leaned back and pulled him into the water.

Seán came up coughing and swearing. "I'll get you for that!"

Laughing, Susan swam for the far side of the pool. "You'll have to catch me first!"

* * *

Inside the villa, Carol was giving Keith and Gemma their lunch.

"Why do we have to go home today, Mammy?" Keith asked.

"There was a mistake. Your Daddy booked the villa for last week and this week, instead of this week and next week, then he forgot which weeks he'd booked."

"Oh." Keith examined his plate. He didn't like his sandwiches; Gemma's lunch looked a lot better. "Where's Daddy now?"

"He's gone to the travel agent to try and change the tickets," Carol said.

"But why do we have to go home *today*?" Keith whined.

Gemma thumped him in the shoulder. "Because, stupid, someone *else* is coming tomorrow."

"Mammy! She hit me!"

"Gemma, don't hit your brother."

Gemma kicked him under the table.

"She kicked me!"

Gemma looked shocked. "I did *not*! Mammy, he's telling lies!"

Keith tried to pull Gemma's hair. "I am not telling lies! You kicked me!"

Carol glared at them. "Right! That's enough. For the rest of this holiday we are going to try and be civilised to each other, okay?"

"Yes, Mammy." Under the table, Keith pinched Gemma's leg.

* * *

Outside in the pool, Susan and Seán were listening to the shouts and screams. Seán laughed. "We only had to put up with those two for a week! Carol must be driven mad."

"I don't envy her one bit," Susan said. "Imagine having to deal with little brats like that *and* Brian every day. Not to mention Billy, who's not the world's most tactful person."

"I wonder how Julie's getting on with Brian," Seán said.

"We should call her before we go. Let her know that we're coming back early."

Seán thought about it. "Nah. It'll be a surprise. God knows, after spending two weeks with Brian she probably needs some cheering up."

* * *

Despite everything that had happened, Julie insisted that

she and Brian continue with their studies. On Friday morning, they returned to *Macbeth*.

"I must know this bloody thing off by heart by now," Brian grumbled.

"Really?" Julie said. "What are the names of Duncan's sons?"

Brian stared at his cousin and the moody expression on his face slowly drooped into an expression of panic. "Em . . . Fleance and Lennox! No, they're noblemen, or something. Em . . . Malcolm and Donalbain?"

"All right, not bad," Julie said. "Okay, here's an interesting one. This is the sort of question that they give in exam papers. Why did Macbeth have Banquo killed?"

"Because Macbeth knew that Banquo knew about the witches and their prophesies, and therefore Banquo knew that Macbeth killed Duncan to become king, like the witches said."

Julie tapped her pencil against her teeth. "Are you sure?"

Brian nodded. "Yep. There's no doubt about that." He sat back with a smug grin fixed on his face.

"And that's what you'd write on an exam paper?"

"More or less. I'd flesh it out a bit, quote a few bits so that the examiner would know I understood the play. But I don't have to do that here, because you know that I understand it."

"Well, if you understand it so well," Julie said, "then tell me what the witches said would happen to Macbeth." "They said he'd become Thane of Cawdor and then king. Soon after, Macbeth is made Thane of Cawdor, so he knows they're telling the truth, then he –"

Julie interrupted him. "Yes, I know you know all that,

but what else did they tell him? Come on, we went through this before, remember? Banquo, and all that? At the banquet table? Hello? Earth to Brian?"

"Give me a minute, I'm thinking about it." Brian shrugged. "They said that he won't have any heirs, but Banquo will."

"So?"

"So *that's* why Macbeth has Banquo killed! To try and stop that part of the prophesy!"

Julie shook her head. "Well, you'll be fine as long as I'm in the exam hall with you."

"You know," Brian said, "this ghost of ours . . . do you really think it's from the future?"

"I don't know. It was only an idea."

"Well, Grandad and Phil seemed to think you were on to something."

"And you don't?"

Brian shook his head. "No. The future can't be changed. Look, imagine someone is killed, and their ghost comes back to prevent it happening, and it succeeds, then that person doesn't die, so their ghost can't come back."

"Yes, but if that happens, then the ghost doesn't *need* to come back."

"All right, take it further then. If the ghost doesn't come back, it can't change the future, so that person *does* get killed. Now do you see what I'm getting at?"

"Ah," Julie said. "You've got a point."

"I'm an expert on time travel," Brian said. "I've watched the *Back to the Future* trilogy dozens of times."

"It's well for those who have a video, being able to

educate themselves like that."

Brian ignored the sarcasm. "I'm pretty sure the ghost is Grandad's mother, all right. This future business is too weird to believe."

"And ghosts aren't? Anyway, it was you who suggested that the ghost wasn't fixed in time, that it was able to visit any time it wanted to. What's it doing here *now* if it is Grandad's mother? Grandad said that the ghost has never made so many appearances in such a short time."

"What really bothers me," Brian said, "is if the ghost *is* someone who hasn't died yet, and it looks like one of the women in the family, then it might be you, or Gemma, or either of our mothers."

"I know," Julie said softly. "I thought of that. I keep hoping I'm wrong about it being someone who dies in the future. Maybe it's true that the ghost just assumes a shape that people will recognise."

"But what would that achieve?"

Julie shrugged. "Nothing. But if the ghost is one of us, then it must be a long time before whoever it is dies, because the ghost changes into an old woman, right? That's another reason why it might be our great-grandmother."

"Yes, but she died when she was only fifty-five. The ghost looked a lot older than that."

"So it could still be any of us," Julie said.

Brian nodded. "I think you're right."

* * *

155

The ghost watched and listened to Julie and Brian as they talked. She was unable to show herself to them or communicate in any way.

Julie, she said to herself, if only I could tell you, warn you, make you understand.

Is Brian right? Is the future unchangeable? I was helped by my future self and, when I visited that time again, I helped my past self. Nothing I could have done could have changed anything. And with Ciarán Kavanagh, I shaped his life, but I only knew about it when he told me as he lay dying. What would have happened if I had not gone back to his past? Would he never have lived in this house? Perhaps he would never have married.

If the future is already written, how can I warn them? How can I help them to help me? There is almost no time left.

Then she remembered the young priest, and the message from her future self: "You must guide him."

* * *

Billy charged into the villa. "Come on! Everyone get your things! There was only one flight I could get for us and it leaves in an hour and a half."

The six of them rushed around the villa, grabbing everything and stuffing their suitcases. Luckily, Carol had already packed most of her things and had instructed Keith and Gemma to do the same.

Seán and Susan were ready first. They phoned for a taxi and helped the others get their things together. While they were waiting for the taxi, the villa's cleaning woman arrived and Susan told her what had happened. She thought the whole thing was hilarious. Her laughter didn't do much to help Billy's mood.

They made it to the airport less than fifteen minutes before the flight was due to leave, then they found that there was a mix-up with the tickets. Billy was close to losing his temper, and Carol kept the children well away from him in case they provoked him too much.

The girl at the ticket desk was extremely apologetic to Billy. "I'm sorry, Mr Doyle, but the travel agent really shouldn't have made that booking."

Billy was raging. "Well, he *did* make that booking, so your company had better honour it!"

Susan could see that Billy's attitude wasn't getting them anywhere. She nudged her husband and whispered "You talk to her, Seán. Use the old charm."

Five minutes later they were on the plane. Susan and Seán had managed to get two seats together near the front, but the others were in single seats scattered throughout the plane.

"Well done," Susan said as she fastened her seatbelt. "What did you say to her?"

"You don't want to know," Seán said, a huge grin spreading across his face.

"I don't think Billy's ever going to talk to you again, Seán. I think he feels that you showed him up in front of his family, and he was in a bad enough mood to begin with."

"Ah, he's a contrary old git. He'd want to watch that temper of his, though. He's liable to get someone killed."

157

* * *

For some reason he couldn't understand, Father McCanney was exhausted. He'd had plenty of sleep the night before and hadn't done anything more strenuous than hold the morning service, but now he couldn't keep his eyes open.

He sat in the armchair in his room, and slowly nodded off to sleep. Half an hour later, he woke screaming from the most vivid and terrifying dream he'd ever had.

A car. Its roof rack was filled with suitcases. There were six people in the car, four adults and two children. The two men were in the front, the one behind the wheel angry, not concentrating on his driving. In the back, the children were overtired and complaining, occasionally fighting. The two women had identical faces, but were wearing different clothes. One wore a light cream jacket, the other a red blouse.

The driver turned around to shout at the children, telling them to behave and shut up. The man in the passenger seat shouted a warning, and the driver turned back in time to see that he was rapidly approaching a red light. He slammed his foot down on the brakes, but something had gone wrong. It made little difference to the car's speed.

The car shot across the junction, swerved to avoid a car coming from the left, and swung across to the wrong side of the road. It smashed into a small car that had stopped for the lights. The smaller car was knocked aside: it overturned and caught fire.

Then the dream had faded out and had been replaced

by a bright hospital room: an operating theatre. Three doctors and four nurses worked frantically around the patient. From his point of view in the dream, Father McCanney only caught a few glimpses of the patient, but it was clear that she was a woman. Her face was badly scarred, and covered with an oxygen mask, but he was certain that it was one of the two women who had been in the car.

Later, when it was over, one of the doctors pulled off his surgical mask and turned away. He walked slowly down the hall to where a group of people were sitting nervously. One of the men jumped to his feet when the doctor approached. The doctor placed his hand on the man's shoulder, and shook his head.

Father McCanney shook as he remembered the dream. It all seemed so real, as though he had seen it happen in real life, as though he'd been in the car and the operating theatre himself.

"I have to write this down," he muttered to himself. "I have to find out if it really happened."

He picked up his notebook and pencil, checked his watch, and noted the time. And as he began to write, he found that he had no control over his hand. It moved the pencil over the page, making deep, dark marks. When it had finished, he stared at the page.

"Help me."

Chapter Eighteen

Father McCanney sat in the darkened confession box. "Say three Hail Marys, and in future try and remember to think before speaking."

"Bless you, Father," the old woman said, then recited the Act of Contrition.

The Priest absolved the old woman's sins and said "Go in peace." He slid the shutter closed and waited silently for someone else to enter the confessional. He smiled to himself as he thought about the old woman. Even though the box had been in darkness, he knew who she was. Her sins were so trivial and she was such a kind-hearted woman that what he really wanted to do was pat her hand and say "I don't blame you, I'd have told her the same thing myself."

He heard the door to the confessional open, and the muffled sounds of someone trying to get comfortable on the kneeling mat. He opened the shutter.

"Bless me, Father, for I have sinned. It has been three weeks since my last confession." It was a young girl's voice. Immediately Father McCanney felt his heart lift. So few young people bothered with confession these days.

"Tell me your sins, my child."

"I've argued with my mother, and I've fought with my grandfather and my cousin." Her voice was wavering, and Father McCanney suspected the girl was on the verge of tears.

"Is there anything else you'd like to tell me?"

The girl sobbed. "Someone I know is going to die! I don't know who, but it's one of us: my mother, or my aunt, or my cousin Gemma. Or it might be me."

The priest's Bible dropped unnoticed to the floor. "Julie! Is that you? This is Father McCanney. I was at your grandad's house."

"Father? Oh, thank God! We saw it again, we saw the ghost again! We think she might be someone who hasn't died yet!"

Father McCanney felt his blood go cold. "Julie, your mother and your aunt. Are they twins? Do they look alike?"

"Yes, Father. They're identical twins."

"We need to talk. Is there anyone else waiting?"

"Just one more, Father."

"Okay. Go to the front of the church, and wait for me. When I'm finished I want to talk to you."

"Aren't you going to give me penance?"

"What? Oh yes. Say three . . . no, never mind. Just talk to God. I think we're going to need His help."

* * *

Father McCanney phoned the villa from the vestry. Julie was standing beside him. She was shaking too much to use the phone herself. "I need to talk to Mr or Mrs Logan," he said.

161

Father McCanney paused to listen. "No, the Logans! From Ireland!" He covered the mouthpiece with his hand. "It's a terrible line. It sounds like she's eating Rice Krispies." He took his hand away. "What? No . . . today? Yes, all right, thank you . . . what? Okay, thank you. Goodbye." He put the receiver back in its cradle.

"They've left already. Apparently your uncle messed up the booking. Someone else has booked the villa for the next two weeks. That was the cleaner, she said that their plane should be landing at about half-past one. That's half two, our time."

"Half two!" Julie said. "We've only got an hour to get to the airport! We've got to stop them from using the car."

Father McCanney chewed on his thumbnail. "I'll phone the airport and leave a message telling them to wait until we get there."

* * *

The Captain's voice crackled over the plane's intercom. "Those of you on the right side of the plane will be just able to make out Dublin bay. We'll be landing in ten minutes, so please keep your seat belts fastened until the plane has come to a complete stop."

"Well, all in all, it wasn't a bad week," Susan said.

"Yeah, it was grand," her husband said. He smiled at her. "You got a bit of a tan. It suits you."

"It's not *that* good a tan, it's just the reflection from my blouse," Susan said. "I can't wait to see Julie. I didn't think I'd miss her that much."

"I know what you mean. Having to stay with those

two screaming kids makes you realise that our Julie's not such a bad lass at all."

Susan gasped. "I've just thought of something! We didn't buy Julie anything!"

Seán patted her hand. "Don't worry, love. She'll understand."

* * *

Marie Hudson picked up the phone in the shop. She cleared her throat and prepared her phone-answering voice. "Hudson's Pharmacy. How may I help you?"

"I'm sorry to trouble you, Mrs Hudson," Julie said. Can I speak to Phil, please?"

"Oh! You must be Julie! Well, it's nice to talk to you at last, dear. Phil's told me so much about you. How are you then, all right?"

"Fine, thanks. Em . . . is he there at the moment? This is sort of important."

"I think he's upstairs, dear. Hold on, I'll call him." She put the phone on hold, and shouted. "Philip! Phone! It's Julie!"

Phil came charging down the stairs and into the shop. "Thanks!" He grabbed the phone. "Julie?"

"Phil, thank God! Look, I don't have time to explain. Can you get your mother's car and drive to my grandad's house and pick up Brian, then come and meet me at the church? It's an emergency!"

"What? Yes, all right. Em . . . what's happened?"

"*Now,* Phil! Please!"

"Okay. Right. I'll see you soon." He put down the receiver and stared at it for a few seconds, then took a deep breath. "Mam, I need to use the car."

* * *

Julie had phoned Brian and told him of the situation and he was waiting at the gate when Phil pulled up.

On the way to the church, Brian told Phil what had happened. "What about your grandad?" Phil asked. "What are you going to tell him?"

"I've left him a note. I just said that you were taking us for a drive. If we're lucky, this will all be over before he even gets home."

Phil drove in silence for a while, then said "Look, if the ghost *is* from the future, do you think we can really change things?"

"I don't know," Brian said. "I had a long talk with Julie about that. We'll just have to try."

* * *

Billy Doyle was in an even worse mood by the time the plane had landed. As they walked to the baggage reclamation area, Keith and Gemma were crying and Carol was trying to keep them quiet.

"All I need now," Billy said to Seán, "is to have the customs officials decide they don't like the look of us."

"Listen, Bill," Susan said. "Thanks for taking us. We really do appreciate it."

But he wasn't listening. Billy turned around and grabbed Keith's hand. "Come on! And stop crying, or I'll give you something to really cry about!"

Susan looked at Seán and smiled. He took her hand and they walked faster, pretending that they didn't notice the scenes of family conflict behind them.

For a change, luck seemed to be with them. Their bags were among the first off the carousel and they loaded them on to a trolley and wheeled it towards the blue customs area.

The single surly customs officer ignored them as they passed and went out into the arrivals terminal.

People waiting for friends and relatives looked at the Logans and the Doyles hopefully as they came through the sliding doors, and then ignored them when they realised it wasn't who they were waiting for.

"Right," Billy said. "Let's get the car, then."

Billy spent five minutes fishing through his pockets and wallet for the carpark ticket, then fed it into the machine and paid the twelve pounds. They pushed the trolley out to the long-term carpark, located their car and loaded the suitcases on to the roof rack.

They all climbed into the car, but just as Billy was about to turn the key in the ignition, Gemma began to cry.

"What's the matter, honey?" her mother asked.

"I have to go to the toilet."

Billy thumped the steering wheel. "Oh, for God's sake! Why didn't you say so before we left the airport?"

Susan opened the car door. "I'll bring her in. We'll only be a few minutes, Bill. Come on, love."

* * *

Inside the terminal, Susan looked around but couldn't find a sign pointing to the toilets. She brought Gemma over to the information desk. "Excuse me," she said to the young man at the desk.

165

He held up his hand. "Just a minute." He walked over to the microphone. His voice interrupted the background music. "Would Mister or Mrs Logan, travelling from Spain, please come to the information desk in the arrivals hall?"

Susan jumped. "Oh! That's me! I'm Mrs Logan."

The young man looked at her. "At last! Didn't you hear the message before?"

"No, we just went straight out. What's the problem?"

"I have a message here from your daughter. She says she's coming to the airport to meet you, and you're to wait for her. She said that whatever happens, you're not to use the car."

Susan frowned. "That's strange . . . how did she know we were coming home early?"

The young man shrugged and returned to his work. Susan felt a tug on her sleeve. She looked down and saw Gemma's pleading eyes. "Excuse me," Susan said to the young man, "where are the toilets?"

He pointed with his pen. "Down there, to the left."

"Thanks."

* * *

As usual, Billy Doyle was furious. "This is ridiculous! Why on earth shouldn't we use the bloody car?"

Susan let out an angry breath. "Look, I don't know. Julie's message just said that we were not to use the car. It didn't say why. I phoned Dad's place, but there was no answer."

"Well, I say we should just wait for her," Seán said.

"I'm sure they won't be long, and then she'll let us know what's the matter."

"They're right, Billy," Carol said. "Waiting another hour or two won't kill us. We're still home a week early as it is."

Billy turned to his wife. "Oh, that's right. Keep rubbing it in, why don't you? Damn it, one bloody mistake and I'm going to keep hearing about it for the rest of my life."

"Oh, for crying out loud, Bill!" Seán said. "What's the big deal? Look, Julie wouldn't have left the message unless she thought it was important. Let's just go back inside, get something to eat, and wait. We can try phoning the house every half-hour, just in case."

Billy looked at the carpark ticket in his hand. "But I've already paid this! They only give you ten minutes to leave, before you have to pay again."

Seán glared at him. "Well, if that's all you're bloody worried about, *I'll* pay it. What's it going to cost, an extra fiver?" He reached into his pocket and took out his wallet.

Billy turned away in disgust. "I don't need *your* charity, Logan."

Inwardly, Seán counted to ten. "All right. Okay. Whatever you say. But let's just go inside and calm down, all right?"

Reluctantly, Billy agreed to wait. They unloaded their suitcases and made their way back into the airport, pushing the luggage trolley ahead of them.

* * *

"How much farther now?" Julie asked.

167

"About another half-hour," Phil said. "Sorry, I'd go faster but we're pushing the speed limit as it is."

Julie grabbed Brian's wrist and looked at his watch. "The plane should have landed by now," she said. "I hope they got the message."

Father McCanney turned around and smiled at her. "Don't worry, Julie. I'm sure they did. Everything's going to be fine."

Brian looked around at the others. "I hope so. Father, about that dream you had . . . what sort of car was it?"

"I don't know, Brian. I'm not much good at guessing the makes of cars." He paused, then said, "And I don't think we should try. We don't want to scare ourselves any more than need be, okay?"

"But from what you said, it definitely *was* my dad's car. I mean, two men, two women who are very alike, a young boy and a girl . . ."

"Brian," Phil said quietly. "Stop, please."

Brian shook his head. "No, we need to talk about this. Father, you said that in your dream, in the operating room, the woman died, then the doctor went out and spoke to one of the men. Which one was he? What did he look like?"

Julie put her hands over her ears. "I don't want to hear this! Brian, shut up!"

* * *

Billy Doyle had taken to pacing around the airport's large cafeteria. From their table, the others watched him carefully.

"Look at him," Seán said. "He's like a tiger in a cage.

The man can't relax for a minute."

Carol and Susan glanced at each other. "He's going to blow his top any second," Carol said. "God, I hate it when he gets like this."

"Does he do it often?" Sean asked.

"No, he hardly ever loses his temper. But when he does, the whole world knows about it."

"Do you want me to talk to him?"

"Better not, Seán," Susan said. "It'll only make things worse."

Billy marched over to the table. "Look, I'm sick of waiting. Susan, do you want to phone your father's place again?"

"I just phoned five minutes ago, Billy."

"Well, phone *again*, damn it!"

Sean stood up suddenly. "All right. Now you just calm down, Bill. You won't help things by shouting at everyone. You're upsetting Susan and Carol, you're scaring the children and – to be honest – you're beginning to get on my nerves. So sit down, shut up, and wait."

Billy suddenly grinned. "Seán, don't you *ever* tell me what to do."

"And don't you ever shout at my wife again."

The two men glared at each other for a full minute, then Billy took a deep breath, and turned to Carol. "You stay here if you want. I'm taking the car, and I'm going home. You can get a taxi or something, when you're ready."

And, with that, he walked away.

* * *

169

Grandad Tom pushed open the hall door. "I'm home!" he called. He listened to the silence, then muttered "and it looks like I'm the only one who is."

He hung up his coat and put away his umbrella, then ambled into the kitchen to make himself a cup of tea. He stood looking out of the window while he waited for the kettle to boil and, as he stared, he became aware that he could see a shape reflected in the glass.

Tom turned around slowly, and stared at the shimmering apparition. The hairs on the back of his hands were standing up, and he felt his heart miss a beat.

"Oh, my God. After all these years . . . tell me," Tom said, his voice barely a whisper. "Who are you?"

The ghost stepped closer, and reached out her hand. Automatically, Tom raised his hand to meet it, but could feel nothing.

"Tell me," he said again.

She raised her hand further, and placed it on his forehead.

And Tom Kavanagh suddenly *knew* why she had haunted his house for so many years. He saw, through her eyes, the ghost's first meeting with his father Ciarán, and her second meeting with him, when she had watched him die. He saw his mother's death, and the births of his twin daughters. He saw the birth of his granddaughter, and then . . . he saw the future, and when he saw the image of Julie as an older woman, tending to her dying mother, the tears began to build in his eyes.

And Tom Kavanagh cried when he realised who the ghost was.

CHAPTER NINETEEN

"Another couple of minutes now," Phil said. "The motorway's just coming up."

"You aren't supposed to go on the motorway," Father McCanney said. "You're a learner driver."

Phil glanced at him and smiled. "I don't think anyone would mind, Father. Not considering the circumstances. Besides, I won't be going too fast."

The car pulled up at a red light.

"I *hate* these lights," Brian said. "They take ages. At least we're first in the queue."

Phil nodded absently and pointed ahead. "Look at that maniac. He must be doing nearly a hundred!"

They all looked towards the car. It was speeding down the motorway, and showed no signs of stopping.

Father McCanney suddenly gasped. "Oh my God! The dream!" He scrambled for his seatbelt.

At the same time, Brian almost screamed. "That's my dad's car!"

"Get out!" Father McCanney shouted. "Get out of the car!" He pushed open the door and ran.

Brian dived over the front seat and scrambled out, just as Phil was undoing his belt.

"Come on, Julie!" Phil shouted, leaping out of his seat.

Julie panicked. She couldn't find the lever to tilt the driver's seat forward.

Ahead, Billy's car began to swerve. The red light was just seconds away. The cars to the right began to move.

Phil reached into the car and grabbed Julie's arm, and pulled.

* * *

Billy Doyle screamed. His right foot was pumping the brake as hard as possible, but it made no difference. Just ahead, at the junction, a car began to move out in front of him. Billy pulled the wheel to the right, and sped around the other car.

Directly in front of him he saw a young man trying to pull a girl out of a stalled car. He tried to swerve again, but the steering wheel slipped in his sweaty hands.

His car skidded, turned, and collided with the other car.

* * *

When the phone rang, Tom almost jumped with shock. He picked it up, his hands still trembling. "Hello?"

"Tom! Thank God you're in! It's Seán, we've been phoning for ages. Listen, is Julie there?"

"No. No . . . I'm not sure where they are. There's a note here saying that . . . that they're gone for a drive."

"Tom, is everything all right?"

Tom swallowed. "No, Seán, it's not." He took a deep breath. "Are you at the airport?"

"Yeah. How did you know?"

"Sean, just stay there. Please. Don't let anyone use Bill's car. There's something wrong with the brakes." He paused. "I . . . believe that Julie and Brian are on their way there to meet you."

"What's happened, Tom? Are you all right?"

"I'm fine. Seán, just wait for Julie. Please. Just wait for her." He hung up, and stared at the phone. "And pray that she gets there safely."

* * *

The young policewoman listened carefully as Father McCanney told her what had happened. He left out any reference to the ghost, and his dreams, and simply said that they'd decided to surprise the others at the airport.

The policewoman took careful note of everything the priest said, but she was clearly disturbed by the story.

Eventually, she said "This is awful. Her own uncle . . ." she turned and looked at the wrecked cars. "It could have been so much worse."

The priest nodded. "If Mr Doyle's car had been full, the extra weight might have prevented the car from stopping as quickly as it did." He smiled. "Even so, it's a miracle no one was hurt."

Father McCanney turned towards Julie, Phil and Brian, and waved. Then he said to the policewoman, "I suppose there's no chance of a lift to the airport?"

CHAPTER TWENTY

After Julie and Brian had finished telling their story, Seán Logan stood up and declared that he was going for a walk to clear his head. He asked Father McCanney to accompany him. The priest declined at first, but Seán insisted.

The two men went up the escalator to the airport's departure area, and then up again to the small bar overlooking the runways. Seán ordered himself a glass of Guinness. "Will you have a drink, Father?" Sean asked.

The priest shrugged. "An orange juice, thanks."

They took their drinks to a small table near the window. "So," Seán said, "This is all serious, then? Not just some wild story?"

"I only wish it *was* made up, Mr Logan. But that dream I had was so real. Everyone in the car was dressed exactly as they are now, even yourself. There's no way I could have known anything like that."

"And you even knew about the faulty brakes on the car?"

Father McCanney nodded. "Yes. In the dream, Mr

174

Doyle slammed down on the brake pedal and it didn't make any difference to the car's speed."

Sean sipped at his drink thoughtfully, then licked the foam moustache from his upper lip. "Last Saturday, when we were driving to Tom's house to say goodbye, we arrived late. Did Julie or Brian mention anything about that?"

The priest frowned. "No . . . should they have?"

"Well, for one thing, Billy's never, *never* late. You could set your clock by him. I think that's one of the reasons he was so upset at messing up the holiday booking. It showed him to be less then perfect, and God knows Billy wouldn't want anyone to think that. Anyway, the reason we were late is because we stopped at a garage to get the brakes checked. There was something wrong with them."

"I see. To be honest, Mr Logan, that doesn't surprise me in the least. There's something else, though. Something I didn't tell Julie or Brian."

"Oh? And what would that be?"

"Well, in my dream, I thought that one of the twins was killed. Of course, I wasn't sure which, and even after telling Julie about it, that still didn't help. Her description of her mother applied to both of them, naturally. The thing is . . ."

"What?"

"Later in the dream, I saw everyone in the hospital. The doctors were working to save someone's life. They failed. One of the doctors walked out, to tell someone about the death. It was *you* he approached."

Seán almost dropped his drink. "Susan . . ."

Father McCanney shook his head. "No. I thought so

at first. But after the accident I began to think back to the dream. I don't know why I didn't remember it at first . . . both your wife and your sister-in-law were in the waiting-room. I think that the woman who died was Julie. I just thought you should know that."

Seán nodded. He stared out the window for a long time, absently watching the planes arrive and depart. Then he turned back to the priest. "Listen, Father . . . I know it's a sin to tell a lie, but there's something I want you to do . . ."

* * *

In the restaurant, Carol Doyle and Susan Logan were still in a mild state of shock. "But what proof do we have of any of this?" Carol asked.

Brian answered her. "Well, apart from three pieces of fairly shaky handwriting and two wrecked cars, no proof at all."

Susan patted Julie's hand. "You must have been scared."

"Terrified," Julie said. "I don't know what we'd have done if Phil hadn't been there."

Phil blushed and said nothing. Susan smiled at him. "I hope your mother understands about you taking the car. And about what happened to it."

"I told her it was an emergency, but I didn't explain exactly what. I didn't even know what was happening myself until Brian told me."

Still white from shock, Billy Doyle turned to Phil. "Listen, son, don't worry about your mam's car. My insurance will take care of it." He leaned forward and put his head in his hands. "God, I've been so *stupid*." Billy looked up. "I am so sorry about this. Brian, Julie, I could have killed you."

Julie stared at her uncle, unsure of what to do. Then she got up from her seat and walked over to him. She wanted to hit him, slap him, somehow hurt him for the damage he might have done. She wanted to lash out at him with all the fear, anger and frustration that had been building up for the past week.

Then she saw his eyes, and she realised that she had seen that expression before: when she'd told Brian how she really felt about his father.

Julie's anger towards her uncle suddenly disappeared, and was replaced with a kind of sadness; she felt sorry for Billy, someone who could only see the world from his own point of view.

She sat down beside him. "I can't blame you for something that didn't happen, Billy." She paused, then added "You were always good to us, when we were kids."

Julie looked over to Brian. He caught her eye, then nodded and smiled.

* * *

Throughout the conversation, Keith and Gemma had sat silently eating their burgers. They hadn't fully understood what was going on, but had been aware that it was important. Now, with the crisis past and everyone in relatively good moods, they were becoming restless.

"I want to go home. I'm bored," Keith said.

"Me too," Gemma said. "I'm more bored than you are."

177

Julie smiled at them. "Do you want to come and watch the planes taking off?"

The children jumped out of their chairs and ran over to her. "Can we, Mammy?"

Carol smiled. "Sure, go ahead."

Julie stood up and grabbed her bag. "Phil? Brian? Are you coming?"

After they had left, Carol turned to Susan. "Julie's young man seems very nice."

Susan nodded. "I like him. He sort of reminds me of Seán when he was that age."

They sat silently for a while, then Susan said, "Do you think it's all true?"

"With luck we'll never find out."

Seán Logan and Father McCanney arrived back from the bar. Seeing Billy, the priest looked at Seán, who nodded. Then the priest said "I need to talk to you, Mister Doyle," and led Billy away.

"What's all that about, Seán?" Carol asked.

He shrugged. "I don't know. Just a sermon, I think. You know the way priests are."

In the distance, Seán could just about hear the priest saying "I notice that your wife's wearing a cream jacket, Mister Doyle," then they had gone too far for Seán to hear them. He smiled to himself. A little white lie from the priest might do a lot of good for Billy Doyle.

* * *

It was almost six o'clock when the taxis dropped them off at Tom Kavanagh's house. "My mother's going to have a fit about the car," Phil said.

"What will you tell her?" Julie asked.

He smiled. "Ah, don't worry, I'll think of something. Though I'll probably be grounded for the rest of my life." He leaned forward, and kissed her gently. "I'll phone you tomorrow, okay?"

Julie realised that her entire family were watching, and she blushed.

"Come on, everyone," Brian said. "Let them say goodbye in peace." He herded the others up the long driveway.

Phil and Julie watched them go. "You going to be okay?" Phil asked.

Julie nodded. "I think so. Thanks for everything, Phil. And I'm sorry about your mam's car."

He shrugged. "It's okay."

"You'll phone me tomorrow?"

"And the day after."

Julie smiled. "And after that?"

Phil returned the smile. "After that? Well, who knows what the future will bring?"

* * *

Considering everything that had happened, Julie's parents had wanted to take her home, but she and Brian insisted that – if it was okay with their grandad – they stay and complete their studies. Later, after the others had gone home, Father McCanney decided it was also time for him to go. Julie thanked him for all that he'd done, but the priest just smiled and shook his head. "I should thank *you*," he said. "For a long time I was looking for a purpose to my life. Father Mitchell will tell you that, he's probably bored sick of hearing me whining. But I know now that no matter how dull or meaningless we might think our lives are, there's still a lot of good we can do."

Julie hugged him. Grandad Tom walked him to the door. "Goodnight, Father McCanney. No doubt we'll see you in Mass on Sunday."

"I hope so, Mr Kavanagh."

The old man smiled. "You can call me Tom. That's what my friends call me."

He waved and watched the priest make his way down the drive. Then he closed the door and returned to the living-room.

"What will you do now that the ghost is gone, Grandad?" Brian asked.

"I'm not sure. I was thinking it might be time for me to retire."

Julie grinned at him. "I'm sure there are other mysteries you could solve."

"Well, I didn't solve this one. *You* did. It had me stuck for years."

"We had a lot of help from the ghost itself," Brian said.

"You mean, the ghost *her*self." He frowned. "I wonder if we'll ever know who it was?"

"I don't think we really need to know," Julie said. She stood up and stretched. "Come on, Brian. Bedtime. We have to get up early and study."

"Speaking of getting up early," Grandad Tom said, "You did a nice job on the garden this morning, Brian. It was well worth a fiver."

Brian grinned and began to collect his things. "I've

learned my lesson. I'm never going to make a bet again."

"It's always been my policy never to make a bet on something I'm not one hundred per cent sure of."

"You're a wise man, Grandad."

"This is true. And do you want to find out how I got to be so wise?"

Brian paused. "Does the answer have anything to do with cutting grass?"

Grandad Tom laughed. "You're too clever by half, young man. Now get to bed."

Julie and Brian said goodnight, and left the room. Tom Kavanagh opened his journal, and spent the next two hours writing down the events of the day. After the last line, he wrote the date and his initials. Then, as an afterthought, he wrote: "I know now that the future is not set. It is shaped by our actions and inactions. When the ghost touched my mind, I saw my own death. It did not appear to be too far in the future: a year, maybe two. However, I know now that it may not come to pass at that time.

"But I know that when it does happen – when I *do* make that final journey – I will be ready."

* * *

Julie sat cross-legged on the bed, writing a letter.

"Dear Maireád,

"How are you? We're having a great time here. Brian's not so bad when you get to know him. Mam and Dad and the others came home today, a week earlier than planned. There was a mix-up with the booking. Anyway, Brian and I will still be staying here for the next two weeks – I have so much news to tell you that I don't know where to begin. Grandad said that you're welcome to come and stay with us for a few days if you like – Brian's very keen to meet you! I think he's a bit jealous because he hasn't got anyone and I've got Phil. Oh! Didn't I tell you about Phil? Silly me, I must have forgotten."

She wrote for another hour, telling Mairéad all about Phil, but she didn't mention the ghost. It was over now, she decided, and perhaps it would be best to try and forget everything that had happened.

Julie had turned out the light and was half-undressed when she noticed that there was a faint glow coming from the mirror.

She stared into the mirror, and where her own reflection should be there was the clear, pale image of a woman . . . She seemed at once both young and old, and Julie felt as though she was seeing the ghost as the person she truly was, at all the stages through her life. Behind the ghost, a grey mist swirled, occasionally illuminated by brief flashes of white light.

The ghost reached her hand out, and placed it on the inside of the glass. "Julie . . ."

Instinctively, Julie put out her own hand and touched the mirror, half expecting to feel flesh instead of glass. "Who are you?"

The ghost smiled. "I don't know if I should tell you that, I'm sorry. I just wanted to thank you, for everything you've done."

"Were we right?" Julie asked. "Are you someone who hasn't yet died?"

"Yes," the ghost said. "as Brian said, time is not fixed for me. I have seen far into the past and the future of this family . . . But there are many possible futures, Julie, and your actions determine how the future will be shaped. You have been clever, and kind, and strong . . . and you have done great work."

Behind the ghost, the pulsating lights began to gather. The ghost glanced at them, then back at Julie.

"And now you're going," Julie said. "Will I ever see you again?"

Again, the ghost smiled. "You will, I can promise you that."

More lights began to gather, coming closer to the other side of the mirror, surrounding the ghost. Behind them, in the distance, one great light outshone them all.

Tears began to build in Julie's eyes. "Please, tell me! Who are you? I have to know!"

The ghost paused, and seemed to look to the surrounding lights for approval. Then she turned back to Julie. "Sometimes it is better not to know these things, Julie. But perhaps for you it would be best if I told you." She gave a gentle laugh. "I wouldn't want you to waste your life worrying about who I might be. If you were to do that, then I might never be born."

Julie suddenly felt almost too weak to stand. "My . . . daughter?"

The ghost turned away quickly, and stared towards the bright light in the distance. "I have to go with them now. He is ready for me."

"He?" Julie asked, fighting back her tears. "Who do you mean?"

The ghost began to move away from the mirror. "He is waiting for me, in the light . . ."

Then Julie suddenly realised. She knew who it was that waited in the light. She had always known. "Is that what I'm seeing now? Is this where everything ends?"

The ghost turned back one last time. "No. This is where everything *begins*." She continued to move away from the mirror, growing fainter with every step.

Julie saw the ghost turn once more towards the light.

And then the image in the mirror – the lights, the mist and the ghost of her daughter – quickly and quietly faded away.

THE END

Other books in the
Dark Shadows
series by Poolbeg

Vampyre by Michael Scott
At the heart of every myth there is a truth . . .
Michael Scott "the king of fantasy in these isles"
ISBN: 1-85371-545-X

Cold Places by Morgan Llywelyn
An exciting fantasy adventure with an
undertone of gradually increasing horror
ISBN: 1-83571-541-7

Blood Brother by JH Brennan
When a demonic entity takes over Seb's
computer, the community is threatened
ISBN: 1-85371-602-2

Shiver!
Fifteen ghostly stories from some of
Ireland's best writers
ISBN: 1-85371-300-7

Chiller
A collection of spine tingling tales from some
of Ireland's leading writers
ISBN: 1-85371-512-3